VIGILES

LEVI W. COOK

WESTBOW®
PRESS
A DIVISION OF THOMAS NELSON
& ZONDERVAN

Scripture quotations are from The Holy Bible, English Standard Version® (ESV®), copyright © 2001 by Crossway, a publishing ministry of Good News Publishers. Used by permission. All rights reserved.

WestBow Press books may be ordered through booksellers or by contacting:

WestBow Press
A Division of Thomas Nelson & Zondervan
1663 Liberty Drive
Bloomington, IN 47403
www.westbowpress.com
1 (866) 928-1240

Because of the dynamic nature of the Internet, any web addresses or links contained in this book may have changed since publication and may no longer be valid. The views expressed in this work are solely those of the author and do not necessarily reflect the views of the publisher, and the publisher hereby disclaims any responsibility for them.

Any people depicted in stock imagery provided by Thinkstock are models, and such images are being used for illustrative purposes only. Certain stock imagery © Thinkstock.

ISBN: 978-1-4908-4740-5 (sc)

Library of Congress Control Number: 2014914939

Printed in the United States of America.

WestBow Press rev. date: 8/22/2014

S tanding on the street corner, he could feel the beginning of a cold fall day. He felt compelled to preach the Word but no one seemed to listen. People walked by him without even a nod or glance in his direction as the wind blew the leaves around him.

Finally, an older gentleman came up to him and with a smirk on his face said, "You preach a lot about the Gospel of Christ. Do you really think we need that in the United States today? We are a country built on the word of God. Everybody knows the story already. You see that church over there? Every Sunday 2,000 people come to hear great music and an encouraging message from our preacher. I don't consider myself a religious man, but I feel good after hearing that man speak from the pulpit. My girlfriend and I live right over there together. We are not married, but we have three kids. Don't preach that stuff about souls being condemned to hell for an eternity that's not what true Christianity is all about. True Christianity is just about loving each other and just doing what feels good. Church doctrine is so 19th century nobody needs that stuff anymore. Why don't you read from a section of scripture that actually has relevance today?"

The gentleman took a step back believing that he had made his point. But he was not standing on this street corner, preaching on this day, to preach what people found pleasing to their ears and not to their hearts. He was here to preach the truth as spoken in scripture. In an age of sexual immorality, homosexuality, and abortion, what could be more relevant then the teachings of scripture? He of all people knew this because even as a believer, even as a young man, he had struggled with his own sinful desires. He had gone astray from his Lord and Savior Jesus Christ. He could see the man wanted a reply, so he searched for a moment in his bible for a passage and he found it. He began reading Ezekiel 16:

"Again the word of the Lord came to me: 'Son of man, make known to Jerusalem her abominations, and say, Thus says the Lord God to Jerusalem: Your origin and your birth are of the land of the Canaanites; your father was an Amorite and your mother a Hittite. And as for your birth, on the day you were born your cord was not cut, nor were you washed with water to cleanse you, nor rubbed with salt, nor wrapped in swaddling cloths. No eye pitied you, to do any of these things to you out of compassion for you, but you were cast out on the open field, for you were abhorred, on the day that you were born.

'And when I passed by you and saw you wallowing in your blood, I said to you in your blood, "Live!" I said to you in your blood, "Live!" I made you flourish like a plant of the field. And you grew up and became tall and arrived at full adornment. Your breasts were formed, and your hair had grown; yet you were naked and bare. When I passed by you again and saw you, behold, you were at the age for love, and I spread the corner of my garment over you and covered your nakedness; I made my vow to you and entered into a covenant with you, declares the Lord God, and you became mine. Then I bathed you with water and washed off your blood from you and anointed you with oil. I clothed you also with embroidered cloth and shod you with fine leather. I wrapped you in fine linen and covered you with silk. And I adorned you with ornaments and put bracelets on your wrists and a chain on your neck. And I put a ring on your nose and earrings in your ears and a beautiful crown on your head. Thus you were adorned with gold and silver, and your clothing was of fine linen and silk and embroidered cloth. You ate fine flour and honey and oil. You grew exceedingly beautiful and advanced to royalty. And your renown went forth among the nations because of your beauty, for it was perfect through the splendor that I had bestowed on you, declares the Lord God.

'But you trusted in your beauty and played the whore because of your renown and lavished your whorings on any passerby; your beauty became his. You took some of your garments and made for yourself colorful shrines, and on them played the whore. The like has never been, nor ever shall be. You also took your beautiful jewels of my gold and of my silver, which I had given you, and made for yourself images of men, and with them played the whore. And you took your embroidered garments to cover them, and set my oil and my incense before them. Also my bread that I gave you—I fed you with fine flour and oil and honey—you set before them for a pleasing aroma; and so it was, declares the Lord God. And you took your sons and your daughters, whom you had borne to me, and these you sacrificed to them to be devoured. Were your whorings so small a matter that you slaughtered my children and delivered them up as an offering by fire to them? And in all your abominations and your whorings you did not remember the days of your youth, when you were naked and bare, wallowing in your blood.

'And after all your wickedness (woe, woe to you! declares the Lord God), you built yourself a vaulted chamber and made yourself a lofty place in every square. At the head of every street you built your lofty place and made your beauty an abomination, offering yourself to any passerby and multiplying your whoring. You also played the whore with the Egyptians, your lustful neighbors, multiplying your whoring, to provoke me to anger. Behold, therefore, I stretched out my hand against you and diminished your allotted portion and delivered you to the greed of your enemies, the daughters of the Philistines, who were ashamed of your lewd behavior. You played the whore also with the Assyrians, because you were not satisfied; yes, you played the whore with them, and still you were not satisfied. You multiplied your whoring also with the trading land of Chaldea, and even with this you were not satisfied.

'How sick is your heart, declares the Lord God, because you did all these things, the deeds of a brazen prostitute, building your vaulted chamber at the head of every street, and making your lofty place in every square. Yet you were not like a prostitute, because you scorned payment. Adulterous wife, who receives strangers instead of her husband! Men give gifts to all prostitutes, but you gave your gifts to all your lovers, bribing them to come to you from every side with your whorings. So you were different from other women in your whorings. No one solicited you to play the whore, and you gave payment, while no payment was given to you; therefore you were different.

'Therefore, O prostitute, hear the word of the Lord: Thus says the Lord God, Because your lust was poured out and your nakedness uncovered in your whorings with your lovers, and with all your abominable idols, and because of the blood of your children that you gave to them, therefore, behold, I will gather all your lovers with whom you took pleasure, all those you loved and all those you hated. I will gather them against you from every side and will uncover your nakedness to them, that they may see all your nakedness. And I will judge you as women who commit adultery and shed blood are judged, and bring upon you the blood of wrath and jealousy. And I will give you into their hands, and they shall throw down your vaulted chamber and break down your lofty places. They shall strip you of your clothes and take your beautiful jewels and leave you naked and bare. They shall bring up a crowd against you, and they shall stone you and cut you to pieces with their swords. And they shall burn your houses and execute judgments upon you in the sight of many women. I will make you stop playing the whore, and you shall also give payment no more. So will I satisfy my wrath on you, and my jealousy shall depart from you. I will be calm and will no more be angry. Because you have not remembered the days of your youth, but have enraged me with all these things, therefore, behold, I have returned your deeds upon your head, declares the Lord God. Have you not committed lewdness in addition to all your abominations?... For thus says the Lord God: I will deal with you as you have done, you who have despised the oath in breaking the covenant, yet I will remember my covenant with you in the days of your youth, and I will establish for you an everlasting covenant. Then you will remember your ways and be ashamed when you take your sisters, both your elder and your younger, and I give them to you as daughters, but not on account of the covenant with you. I will establish my covenant with you, and you shall know that I am the Lord, that you may remember and be confounded, and never open your mouth again because of your shame, when I atone for you for all that you have done, declares the Lord God.'"

But the gentleman cut him off saying; "Jesus never spoke such words that was part of the old covenant. Jesus was all about love."

He answered him with another section of scripture; this one he knew almost by heart. "In Luke 20:9-18, Luke writes "And he [Jesus] began to tell the people this parable: 'A man planted a vineyard and let it out to tenants and went into another country for a long while. When the time came, he sent a servant to the tenants, so that they would give him some of the fruit of the vineyard. But the tenants beat him and sent him away empty-handed. And he sent another servant. But they also beat and treated him shamefully, and sent him away empty-handed. And he sent yet a third. This one also they wounded and cast out. Then the owner of the vineyard said, "What shall I do? I will send my beloved son; perhaps they will respect him." But when the tenants saw him, they said to themselves, "This is the heir. Let us kill him, so that the inheritance may be ours." And they threw him out of the vineyard and killed him. What then will the owner of the vineyard do to them? He will come and destroy those tenants and give the vineyard to others.' 'When they heard this, they said, 'Surely not!' But he looked directly at them and said, 'What then is this that is written: "The stone that the builders rejected has become the cornerstone"? Everyone who falls on that stone will be broken to pieces, and when it falls on anyone, it will crush him.'"

"So if that is the case..." the gentleman said. "...then we are all going to hell." But he answered the gentleman with another passage of scripture this one from John 14:1-21. According to John "Jesus answered, 'Let not your hearts be troubled. Believe in God; believe also in me. In my Father's house are many rooms. If it were not so, would I have told you that I go to prepare a place for you? And if I go and prepare a place for you, I will come again and will take you to myself, that where I am you may be also. And you know the way to where I am going.' Thomas said to him, 'Lord, we do not know where you are going. How can we know the way?' Jesus said to him, 'I am the way, and the truth, and the life. No one comes to the Father except through me. If you had known me, you would have known my Father also. From now on you do know him and have seen him.'

"Philip said to him, 'Lord, show us the Father, and it is enough for us.' Jesus said to him, 'Have I been with you so long, and you still do not know me, Philip? Whoever has seen me has seen the Father. How can you say, "Show us the Father"? Do you not believe that I am in the Father and the Father is in me? The words that I say to you I do not speak on my own authority, but the Father who dwells in me does his works. Believe me that I am in the Father and the Father is in me, or else believe on account of the works themselves.

'Truly, truly, I say to you, whoever believes in me will also do the works that I do; and greater works than these will he do, because I am going to the Father. Whatever you ask in my name, this I will do, that the Father may be glorified in the Son. If you ask me anything in my name, I will do it.

'If you love me, you will keep my commandments. And I will ask the Father, and he will give you another Helper, to be with you forever, even the Spirit of truth, whom the world cannot receive, because it neither sees him nor knows him. You know him, for he dwells with you and will be in you.

'I will not leave you as orphans; I will come to you. Yet a little while and the world will see me no more, but you will see me. Because I live, you also will live. In that day you will know that I am in my Father, and you in me, and I in you. Whoever has my commandments and keeps them, he it is who loves me. And he who loves me will be loved by my Father, and I will love him and manifest myself to him.'"

"So is there more to the whole Christian thing then just going to heaven?" The man asked him. He then read to him Matthew 28:19-20, "Go therefore and make disciples of all nations, baptizing them in the name of the Father and of the Son and of the Holy Spirit, teaching them to observe all that I have commanded you. And behold, I am with you always, to the end of the age."

"Yes but how can you make a claim like that standing on this street corner? Does it not say in the bible that you have to ask permission from an unbeliever before you can share the gospel with them such as in 2 Corinthians 9:13? So by whose authority are you standing here today preaching such things?" He then read to the gentleman 2 Corinthians 10 when Paul writes: "I, Paul, myself entreat you, by the meekness and gentleness of Christ—I who am humble when face to face with you, but bold toward you when I am away!— I beg of you that when I am present I may not have to show boldness with such confidence as I count on showing against some who suspect us of walking according to the flesh. For though we walk in the flesh, we are not waging war according to the flesh. For the weapons of our warfare are not of the flesh but have divine power to destroy strongholds. We destroy arguments and every lofty opinion raised against the knowledge of God, and take every thought captive to obey Christ, being ready to punish every disobedience, when your obedience is complete.

"Look at what is before your eyes. If anyone is confident that he is Christ's, let him remind himself that just as he is Christ's, so also are we. For even if I boast a little too much of our authority, which the Lord gave for building you up and not for destroying you, I will not be ashamed. I do not want to appear to be frightening you with my letters. For they say, "His letters are weighty and strong, but his bodily presence is weak, and his speech of no account." Let such a person understand that what we say by letter when absent, we do when present. Not that we dare to classify or compare ourselves with some of those who are commending themselves. But when they measure themselves by one another and compare themselves with one another, they are without understanding.

"But we will not boast beyond limits, but will boast only with regard to the area of influence God assigned to us, to reach even to you. For we are not overextending ourselves, as though we did not reach you. For we were the first to come all the way to you with the gospel of Christ. We do not boast beyond limit in the labors of others. But our hope is that as your faith increases, our area of influence among you may be greatly enlarged, so that we may preach the gospel in lands beyond you, without boasting of work already done in another's area of influence. 'Let the one who boasts, boast in the Lord.' For it is not the one who commends himself who is approved, but the one whom the Lord commends."

He furthered his remarks by stating to the gentleman. "Sir, I am no Paul but I do proclaim the good news of the gospel of Jesus Christ under the authority of the Holy Spirit which convicts in my heart a call to witness to the whole world what Christ has done and continues to do in my life. I am not ashamed to rise my voice when others wish me silent for the silent Christian who does not proclaim the Gospel and does not go as Jesus according to Matthew 'and make disciples of all men baptizing them in the name of the Father, Son, and Holy Spirit' is no Christian at all but merely a coward and the truth is not in him."

He could see the gentleman a little ways away on his cellphone. 15 minutes later the police arrived and asked him to leave; when he challenged them to name his crime, they said he was being discriminatory against other people and disturbing the peace. But he would not move from his place, so they arrested him and issued him a fine. He spent that night in jail even though he knew the words he spoke were true and just. He remembered the words of John 16: 1-4 when Jesus spoke saying: "I have said all these things to you to keep you from falling away. They will put you out of the synagogues. Indeed, the hour is coming when whoever kills you will think he is offering service to God. And they will do these things because they have not known the Father, nor me. But I have said these things to you, that when their hour comes you may remember that I told them to you."

"He had not moved for hours, and only the coming of night and the rain revived him. He moved, agony in every muscle, anguish in his side, a mighty throbbing inside his skull, but somehow he managed distance. He crawled, walked, staggered, fell. He fainted, then revived, lay for a time mouth open to the rain, eyes blank and empty.

By now his friends believed him dead…Well he was not dead, but he was not going back."

-Louis L'amour *The Skull and the Arrow*

"There is not one among us in whom a devil does not dwell; at some time, on some point, that devil masters each of us; ... but the man who does in the end conquer, who does painfully retrace the steps of his slipping, why he shows that he has been tried in the fire and not found wanting. It is not having been in the Dark House, but having left it, that counts…"

-Theodore Roosevelt
Letter to E.A. Robinson, 27 March 1916

"I saw that everything within my view which ought to be white, and been white long ago, and had lost its lustre, and was faded and yellow. I saw that the bride within the bridal dress had withered like the dress, and like the flowers, and had no brightness left but the brightness of her sunken eyes. I saw that the dress had been put upon the rounded figure of a young woman, and that the figure upon which it now hung loose, had shrunk to skin and bone."

–Charles Dickens *Great Expectations*

"Then I saw a new heaven and a new earth, for the first heaven and the first earth had passed away, and the sea was no more. And I saw the holy city, new Jerusalem, coming down out of heaven from God, prepared as a bride adorned for her husband. And I heard a loud voice from the throne saying, 'Behold, the dwelling place of God is with man. He will dwell with them, and they will be his people, and God himself will be with them as their God. He will wipe away every tear from their eyes, and death shall be no more, neither shall there be mourning, nor crying, nor pain anymore, for the former things have passed away.'"

Revelation 21:1-4 ESV

"I opened to my beloved,
but my beloved had turned and gone.
My soul failed me when he spoke.
I sought him, but found him not;
I called him, but he gave no answer.
The watchmen found me
as they went about in the city;
they beat me, they bruised me,
they took away my veil,
those watchmen of the walls.
I adjure you, O daughters of Jerusalem,
if you find my beloved,
that you tell him
I am sick with love." Song of Solomon 5:6-8 ESV

CHAPTER 1

His men were in position. They had the house surrounded. The cold frigid air of a Williston winter bit furiously at his skin. He had orders to raid the house. The informant said that the drugs and guns were here, but still he felt nervous. It was as if something was off, and he did not know what. He had worked for the ATF a long time. Fear had always been with him, but as he clicked the radio on to give the command to move in, he felt death converging on him.

They crashed down the door, but the house was vacant. No one had been living here for quite some time. He was standing in the living room looking out the window as his men searched. That's when he saw it. He was looking out across the road to the hills in front of him. Someone had lit a large bonfire on one of the hills, but they had arranged the fire in such a way that it spelled out a series of numbers 3-7-77. He could see a figure dressed in a red cape moving towards the house. When the figure got within 20 feet of the house, he raised up his right hand. For one brief moment, he could hear the bomb go off in the house. For one brief moment, he thought of the wife he would never see again. His children he would never hold again. Death had finally found him in the end.

* * *

The street lights grew dim. The air stood still. He could sense the danger. There were only a few other cars besides his in the parking lot. He tightened the grip on the bag of groceries in his left hand as he looked over his shoulder. Even though he couldn't see anybody he knew they were there. His cover had been blown. The only question remained how bad the damage was. He knew the guns were here. The Williston area was the perfect setup. A high population and little to no law enforcement. His contact up until yesterday had been cooperative, but now the man was running scared. Suddenly, a shot rang out and hit the window of the car behind him. Lee spotted the shooter in a black Chevy pickup in front of him. He dropped the groceries and reached for his side arm and fired two rounds into the cab of the pickup killing the man instantly. He turned to his right and saw another man running towards him. He emptied his magazine into the man stopping him in mid-stride. He could hear the screeching of tires and turned back around to his left and saw an orange Corvette speeding out of the parking lot. Lee ejected the spent magazine in his gun as he ran over to where Cace was parked about 100 yards away. Cace hit the gas before Lee even had a chance to close the door.

"If we lose him then my cover is really going to be blown." Lee said as Cace weaved the car in and out of traffic.

The men abruptly came to an icy spot in the road. Lee could hear Cace applying the brakes and watched the Corvette in front of them lose control and go off the shoulder of the road. The vehicle rolled three times before landing face up in a farmer's beet field. Lee and Cace approached the vehicle cautiously, but the driver was already dead.

"Looks like we are heading to Billings." Cace said gesturing to the back of the vehicle.

The vehicle had Billings' plates.

* * *

He walked slowly up to the pulpit. A sea of faces met his gaze as he stared out into the congregation. He opened his bible and began "In Genesis 3:6-7 the author writes, 'So when the woman saw that the tree was good for food and that it was a delight to the eyes, and that the tree was to be desired to make one wise, she took of its fruit and ate and she also gave some to her husband who was with her, and he ate. Then the eyes of both were opened, and they knew that they were naked. And they sewed fig leaves together and made themselves loincloths.' It is interesting that Adam did not rise up and kill the serpent. The representative of mankind willingly chose not to stand up and fight for the bride God had given him. Sin consequently enters the world and Adam and Eve are forced out of the Garden of Eden because of their own folly. My question to you is this 'Where is the hope?' Mankind fails now we as humans are to quote Paul in Ephesians 2:3 are 'children of wrath' and according to what John says in Matthew 3:12 'God's winnowing fork is in his hand, and he will clear his threshing floor and gather his wheat into the barn, but the chaff he will burn with unquenchable fire.' So I will ask you dear Christian where is the hope?"

* * *

The street light flickered on the corner. Jarvis sat in the car waiting and watching for the signal. The bookstore right across the street loomed menacingly before him. He thought the structure itself was large and ugly with its neon lights and gaudy posters plastered to the outside. Cicero said it needed to fall. One man was supposed to clip the wiring in the electrical box outside. Another man was supposed to enter through the back door and plant the device. Jarvis sipped nervously on an energy drink. His heart beat fast. He had never done this before.

Suddenly, the neon lights flickered then darkened completely. Jarvis flipped a U turn in the street and parked the car a few feet from the door. He could hear noises inside. People were talking in hushed tones. The door then opened, and two men climbed into the cab next to him. One of the men told him to drive. Jarvis obeyed. As he pulled away from the bookstore he counted down the minutes inside his head. Five minutes passed before he could hear the explosion.

The two men in the cab beside him said nothing. It was then that he realized his palms were sweaty.

* * *

He started out early. The crisp morning air already beginning to turn sultry and dry. Another hot day. He knew it. Every fiber in his body knew it. Sunscreen, Gatorade, sunscreen, Gatorade. Pulling weeds, watering plants, pulling weeds, watering plants, pruning roses. The job hard, the work painfully repetitive, but he couldn't think of a more useful alterative. The job market in Billings was as dry as the hot air beginning to form around him. He had labored and tried for so long. At the same time he was grateful for the work. After all he did have bills to pay.

Oddly enough, he had the same view when it came to religion and to his faith. He would sit in the pew every Sunday and listen to the pastor preach, but once Monday rolled around he found himself in the same rut he was in the week before. He knew he was a sinner. He knew he needed to change, but he did not know how. He sought answers in the preacher's preaching, but each Sunday the theme was different and did not address the problem that was at hand. One Sunday it was a Cowboy theme. The next Sunday it was a Space Odyssey theme. He felt hungry for something but he did not know what. He felt so far from God.

* * *

He stood on the edge of a large rock face overlooking the city. Night had fallen and the magic had already happened. Everything a glow beneath his feet. Buildings, streetlamps, cars, the river itself seemed to glow as the full moon reflected off the cool pure water of the Yellowstone. There was so much light, and yet there was so much darkness surrounding that light.

Since the day he was born, Lee had known of its presence. Whether it was the verbal and physical abuse from his foster father growing up or the separation from his sister when he was 14, he had often felt it and knew of its mysterious ways better than most. He was as much an outsider as the cowboy that rides the open range, but instead of running away from society he was running towards it to reclaim something that by right was his all along. A thief had come in the night and took his life from him. Parents dead when he was 5. Foster homes, foster homes, foster homes. He left a piece of himself at each of the homes he lived in. Until finally he ran out of things to give, and he became only a shell of a man devoid of any feelings or emotions. Maybe that's why his last foster parents were such a disaster. Perhaps it was as much his fault as it was theirs for what happened that night.

He forced the memory of that aside and focused instead on the assignment. The assignment nobody at the ATF thought he could solve. It could have been a vote of confidence against his mental psyche. After all he had only been discharged from the army 2 years ago, and the ghosts of the war still haunted him, but a lot of water had passed under the bridge since that IED went off and a piece of metal punctured his lung. He was different but stronger this time. He loved to read. One of his favorite books was Herman Melville's *Moby Dick*. Like Ahab an experienced whaler sharpened by the sea, he was sharpened by the world and its cruel ways. Its lessons were itched across his body. Every scar told a story and every wrinkle was a map that connected those stories together. Taken as a whole he was a man bent on getting even with the darkness, and it all started with tonight.

He walked slowly back to his truck steadfast in his resolve. He had to meet a man called Hermes at a coffee shop in 15 minutes. A low level operative for *Vigiles*, a radical terrorist organization responsible for the deaths of 20 people mostly criminals, and 10 ATF agents. *Vigiles* supplied guns to all the wrong people. Crime families, drug smugglers, they helped with political assassinations. The FBI wanted them stopped so did the ATF. It was a joint task force that was being used. Spear headed by Lee and Cace Franklin. Lee represented the ATF, and Cace represented the FBI. Their mission was to find the guns and dismantle the group's underground network of arms dealing. Walking into the coffee shop, Lee felt nervous. Hermes was already sitting at a booth sipping a mocha.

"You're early." He said ordering a double Latte for himself.

"I like coming here." Hermes answered peering up from a book he was reading.

"It's a nice place." Lee confessed.

"You know what makes it nice?" Hermes asked.

"Free Wifi." Lee answered sarcastically.

"Order. Neat precise order."

"Something wrong with order?" Lee asked.

"Depends on how it is achieved. There is order, and then there is the illusion of order. One is achieved by violence, and the other is achieved by laws."

"You don't believe in the law?" Lee asked surprised.

"The law gives the illusion of order to society. Take for example this coffee shop. What is stopping me from pulling out my gun and shooting the barista for neglecting to add the whip cream in my mocha?"

"Words on a slip of paper composed by gray haired old men." Lee answered.

"Wrong. It's the realization that I would not make it out of this coffee shop alive, and if I did I would not last 10 minutes out there before a law abiding citizen would shoot me. Because you see my friend the people of this state believe in the law of the Old Testament. It's the law that governed the old west for years. Bannack, Virginia City, Last Chance Gulch, Helena, and now Billings." Hermes said gesturing towards his book. "Not the superficial laws written by gray haired old men."

"Men create laws to prove to themselves that they are not like the rest of the animals, and that they are the dominant species. They are lying to themselves Lee. There is little difference between man and the rest of the animals in god's holy kingdom. The only difference is we are a lot more creative on how we kill each other." Hermes said finishing his cup of coffee. Rising to leave he gave Lee a pat on the shoulder.

"Come on let's do the lord's work."

* * *

He awoke in a cold sweat. He did not know why he was sweating all he knew was that there was a feeling of death in the air that had not been there before. He knew of death. He felt its presence many times. Once in a meth lab near Havre, a kid working for him was smoking a joint next to some kerosene. "What are you doing?" He had said. The kid merely shrugged his shoulders. "Hey man I'm just doing what feels natural." He left the lab in disgust. A couple minutes later a loud explosion rocked the landscape. He left the area soon after that.

He felt death again while he was helping a friend transport some drugs across the Montana and Idaho border. The highway patrol stopped them about 30 miles from Missoula. "Where are you boys heading?" The patrol man asked. "Friend's birthday party." He had said. The patrol man asked him to step out of the car and walk over to the patrol car. He complied. He remembered watching his friend talk to the officer. He remembered his friend reaching for his registration in the glove box. A shot suddenly rang out. The officer lay dead on the side of the road. They got the merchandise to Missoula then ditched the car.

Death had come to visit him so many times before that he didn't think much of the feeling now. He went to the kitchen and fixed himself a drink. Walking over to the window of his trailer, he peered out onto King Avenue. Suddenly, his eyes caught sight of something written on a telephone pole a hundred yards away. It looked like numbers spray painted black onto the wood. He could just barely make them out. "3-7-77".

A loud blast suddenly rocked the trailer. Flames engulfed the entire structure. A couple hours later local news channels picked up the story. The headline read "House Explosion Cause Unknown."

* * *

Lee and Hermes sat on a park bench watching people go through the fair grounds. Hermes' phone rang. He put it on speaker.

"Is it finished?"

The man on the other end answered "Tell Cicero the explosion went off like clockwork."

"You see Lee…" Hermes said putting away his phone. "…this is my sanctuary. This is the place where I feel the closest to god. He speaks to me. He commands me to carry out his handiwork. Through the darkness there is light and through the light there is hope. I am the hope for this town Lee. You see, like the founding fathers of Billings, I know that we must work through trials and tribulations, but there is only one true leader and that's Cicero. Out of the desert of greed, selfishness, and evil desires, he walked into our lives to bring us peace. You are either with us Lee or against us."

"Well let's go do the lord's work then." Lee answered.

"That's the spirit."

* * *

He was about halfway through the sermon now, and he could tell people were getting anxious to leave but he pressed on. "'Beware of false prophets' Jesus said in Matthew 7:15-20, 'who come to you in sheep's clothing but inwardly are ravenous wolves. You will recognize them by their fruits. Are grapes gathered from thornbushes, or figs from thistles? So, every healthy tree bears good fruit, but the diseased tree bears bad fruit. A healthy tree cannot bear bad fruit, nor can a diseased tree bear good fruit. Every tree that does not bear good fruit is cut down and thrown into the fire. Thus you will recognize them by their fruits.' So if we live in a world like this dear Christian where is our hope?"

CHAPTER 2

H e was dreaming again, and he knew it. His foster father had been dead for 15 years, and yet his face appeared as clear to him now as he lay in bed. He could see his foster father coming into his and Jackie's room. He could hear Jackie scream. A shot rang out, and suddenly he was awake.

Lee climbed slowly out of bed. He knew Cace was going to ask about last night. Last night was organized chaos and who knew what sort of plans the group had for tonight. His phone suddenly vibrated on the nightstand. Flipping open the top he read the text.

Underpass 15 minutes.

Great. Lee thought. What a way to start out a morning. After a quick shower and a shot of OJ he hopped into his pickup and drove across town to the meeting place. He could see Cace's car parked under the underpass. Cace was sitting on his bumper. Cace Franklin a large African American from Harlem. The two men had known each other ever since Lee joined the ATF and jumped at the chance to work with one another. He looked over his shoulder as Lee walked up.

"Well lets have it." Cace said.

"We met at the coffee shop..."

"You and Hermes?"

"...right and then his cellphone rang we went to the fairgrounds and the next thing I know a bomb blast occurs barely 10 minutes later."

"Careful and methodical" Cace said matter factly.

"You don't think they know about Willston do ya?"

"Hard to say."

"Hermes mentioned the name Cicero. Apparently he is like some sort of deranged prophet to these guys. He might even be there at the ceremony tonight."

"I doubt it." Cace answered running his fingers through his hair. "The man's a ghost. He probably doesn't even talk to his own men face to face."

"Do you know where they got the explosives?" Lee asked.

"It's all Betty Crocker style. I'm sure. The same as the bookstore bombing. Leave no trace that's what these guys' are all about."

"Well I better get ready for tonight." Lee said taking a deep breath.

"Remember…" Cace said. "…if it all goes south get out and make your way to the rendezvous point."

* * *

There was that voice way off in the distance. He wasn't even sure he had heard it. Passing through life, he had dismissed the sound as a minor disturbance. The wind running its fingers through the trees. The faint whisper of a deer munching on some roses. It couldn't be real. Could it? He had worked alone by himself for so long he didn't know if he could trust his own senses. It came again that soft gentle rumbling against the sky. Approaching thunderstorm perhaps.

He had a dream once as a boy of being forgotten. He dreamt he awoke and no one was there. His parents, brothers, and sisters no one was in the house where they lived. It was a dream that still haunted him of being forgotten. What sweet joy there is in remembrance he thought as he walked over to weed the next bed. Do you still remember me, or have I forgotten you? He listened again but could not hear the voice in the distance calling out to him. A hawk stood upon a gazebo and watched him intently.

* * *

Lee made his way down 6th Avenue just past the fairgrounds.

He turned into the center lane as he waited for the light to change. He then made his way down 1st Ave. North. The old Pierce Meatpacking building loomed menacingly to his left. The building itself was actually multiple buildings combined into one large conglomerate mess of brick, concrete, and steel. The original building stood in the center of a lot with the words **Pierce Packing Co.** painted across one side of its brick face. A labyrinth of concrete buildings that were added on during the many stages of the company's long history surrounded the original structure. A set of railroad tracks ran parallel to it on the south complimented by a large steel silo that jutted out of one of the concrete buildings. Some of the buildings were constructed back in the 1920s and had not been used since 1983 when a hazardous chemical spill contaminated millions of pounds of meat. The majority of the buildings were seldom used anymore and stood merely as nostalgic reminders of an era long since forgotten in the city's history.

He drove a little past the structures before he parked the truck down a side street about a block away. Taking the pistol from the glove box he ejected a shell into the chamber.

"You must be washed in the blood of the righteous before you can stand with men like Cicero." Hermes had told him in the park. "We are all filthy creatures with harmful tendencies. Those tendencies must die inside you before you can become one of the reborn."

Lee wondered what bizarre little ritual was going to play out here tonight. He took a deep breath as he made his way to the front of the building. All of these people should be on couches taking tranquilizers. He thought to himself. He made his way up the steps before entering the warehouse. Inside darkness greeted him. He could not see or hear anything, but he knew others were there just as a man senses someone standing beside him without seeing them. He sensed people all around him. Until suddenly he found himself in the midst of strangers. There was a faint glow coming from the far end of the warehouse, and Lee found himself being ushered over to it. A single candle emitted a faint light and behind that candle stood a figure cloaked in some red garment. The figure wore a hood, so Lee could not see a face. Lee could see that the figure was holding something in its right hand. As he got closer he could see that the object was an axe. Fear engulfed him. Was he discovered? Were they going to kill him? Should he resist? He still did not know how many more people were in the warehouse. There could be two or three or there could be three hundred. He simply did not know and that's what held his fear in check as the unseen hands beckoned him to the hooded phantom in red.

He got to within five feet of the phantom and he could see part of the figure's face beneath the cloth. It was a man. Lee could barely make out the faint stubble of a beard, but the stranger's eyes were hidden from him.

"Kneel." The stranger commanded.

Reluctantly, Lee got down on his knees. He could feel death surrounding him. This was it. The end of the line. The last hurrah. So this is how Custer felt. Lee mused. Humor kept his fear in check now. There was a certain finality that filled his soul in this moment. He could see the stranger raising the axe. He waited for the blow, but it never came. A warm moist liquid poured over his body. Blood. But he did not feel any pain. Maybe the stranger missed his head and hit him someplace else. He heard a jingle noise above him. Looking up he could see a cow's carcass hanging from the ceiling. He could hear the stranger's voice as it pierced the darkness.

"Your blood is now no longer your own but is the blood of your brothers and sisters. You are now a marked man. Your life is no longer your own. Your mission the mission of vengeance which is the sister of justice. From this day forth she will be your guide. A patron saint that you will pray to. Surely, goodness and mercy will not follow you all the days of the life you now lead. Instead the cold winds of darkness with follow you all the days of your life, and you will dwell in the house of destruction forever, but you will be the instrument of that destruction. For in this world there are many walls and many false idols that need to be torn down and destroyed, and you can destroy them with the hammer of vengeance. Only when the dust settles can a new kingdom be born. And when that day comes you will take your place among god's special elite and then even the angels will jealously proclaim your deeds. Arise dear brother and embrace your destiny."

Lee slowly rose to his feet and came face to face with the man he now knew was Cicero.

* * *

When he started out this morning, the fog had already settled over the farmers' fields. It gave the landscape around him a surreal look that reminded him of an old horror movie. He didn't believe in werewolves, but he couldn't help letting his mind wander as he drove slowly down the road.

The fog would soon pass, but the dream he had last night would stay with him forever. He dreamt he was in a large mansion with ceilings that seemed to stretch to the sky. He was in one of the room's of the mansion when he heard a voice speak to him.

"This is my master's house go and make sure all the doors are open."

He thought this request odd but he complied. Trying each door he came to he found them unlocked, and he opened them. Some of the doors were small some were large. Some felt heavy and were hard to open while others felt light to the touch. But he opened them all save for one. Try as he might he could not get this door open. Suddenly, the voice came to him again.

"My master is here. Why haven't you opened the door?"

But before he could explain he awoke from the dream. What did it all mean? What was behind that door?

* * *

He continued on further in the sermon. "If we cannot measure up to God on our own and we know that we need to give everything to

13

him. Where is our hope? Jesus said in Mark 12:43-44 when talking about the widow who gave two small coins, 'Truly, I say to you this poor widow has put in more than all those who are contributing to the offering box. For they all contributed out of their abundance, but she out of her poverty has put in everything she had, all she had to live on.' But is this woman's money enough to get her into heaven and if not then what must she do? Where is the hope dear Christian?"

* * *

Lee sat in his truck at the gas station.

It had taken him a long time to find her, but there she was sitting in his lap. The file opened before him read *Jackie Marie Cash born Dec. 3 1984.* According to the file, she had been in and out of foster homes until she got her life straightened out and became a cop. A cop. Suddenly, Lee felt an overwhelming sense of pride sweep over him. His sister a police officer for the city of Billings. All these years since his parents' death Lee feared that his sister was dead or that he would never find her. Yet there she was still as sweet and beautiful as ever. The file said she lived alone in an apartment complex off of King Ave.

He was flipping through the radio in his truck when he came to one station where a pastor was speaking: "Remember the words of the prophet Isaiah when he said 'A voice of one calling: in the desert prepare the way for the Lord; make straight in the wilderness a highway for our God. Every valley shall be raised up, every mountain and hill made low; the rough ground shall become level, the rugged places a plain. And the glory of the Lord will be revealed, and mankind together will see it.'" Man that wasn't what I was told last night. Lee mused. He had already taken five showers, and he still could not get rid of that foul stench. I truly am a marked man.

CHAPTER 3

The long day had drawn to an inevitable conclusion, and he once again found himself alone at the nursery. Standing in the midst of a long row of seedless cotton woods nestled in their large black pots he had that feeling of being watched. He wasn't sure what was out there, but his senses told him there was something. It was as if a shadow was passing over him. The sun momentarily blotted out. The annoying killdeer in the fields hushed. As if the footsteps of God himself were trodding on men's souls. But was it really God that was out there? Or something else? He couldn't help but be reminded of Job 7:1-6 when Job states, "Has not man a hard service on earth, and are not his days like the days of a hired hand? Like a slave who longs for the shadow, and like a hired hand who looks for his wages, so I am allotted months of emptiness, and nights of misery are apportioned to me. When I lie down I say, 'when shall I arise?' But the night is long, and I am full of tossing till the dawn. My flesh is clothed with worms and dirt; my skin hardens, then breaks out afresh. My days are swifter than a weaver's shuttle and come to their end without hope."

* * *

It was Friday morning, and Jackie could feel Mark's body next to her. Even though they were not married they had made love to each other last night. Jackie had been to church many times and knew that it was wrong, but she longed for these moments. Moments were she actually felt loved. Moments were she actually felt something anything. Often times whether she was at work or at home she would feel so hallow, so empty as if a piece of her was missing. Sammy would often fill that void for her as only a child can, but Sammy was staying at a friend's house and Jackie hated feeling alone. She met Mark at Perkins' right after she was done with her shift. The two of them had a nice quiet dinner and then drove back to Jackie's apartment.

Joining the department was like a dream come true for Jackie. Ever since she was in high school she wanted to become a cop. Greg her foster father would take her down to the courthouse every Saturday, and they would eat lunch at the park. There was a monument that stood on the south corner of the park. It was constructed in remembrance of James T. Webb, the city's first sheriff to get killed in the line of duty. Jackie used to love reading the inscription on the monument that read:

James T. Webb Sheriff of Yellowstone County
Sealed Duty with His Life March 24 A.D. 1908
A Community's Tribute to Faithfulness.

The words seemed so sacred to her even though she knew little about the man. Honor was still honor. Faithfulness was still faithfulness. A common language spoken by all people who value their community and serve. But did she know what true honor and faithfulness was?

Those days in the park were some of the few happy days of her life. In and out of foster homes for this or that she grew up feeling apart from everyone else. She had a brother at one time or another but who knows where he was now. The two of them were separated and put into different foster homes after Lee...The images of that night still haunted her. She was only 11 at the time. Lee almost 16. She remembered her foster father coming into the room that she and Lee shared. She remembered her foster father telling Lee to leave the room. When Lee refused, a fight ensued between foster father and foster son. Her foster father's gun went off. That's all she remembered about that fateful night.

Jackie got out of bed. Putting on her robe she went into the kitchen to make some coffee. It looked like she was out of coffee. Fumbling around in the cabinets above the sink for about 10 minutes, she finally found a half a bag of Folgers tucked in the back behind the plastic cups. It was a little chiller in the kitchen than normal, and Jackie noticed that the door to the apartment was slightly ajar. Did Mark forget to close and lock the door last night? Suddenly, panic swept over her. Her senses were suddenly alert. Jackie walked slowly back to her bedroom closet and got her .380 pistol. Mark was still asleep, and Jackie decided not to wake him in case this turned out to be nothing.

Jackie slowly made her way into the living room. She made a slow scan of the room before making her way to the ajar door. Keeping the pistol pointed in front of her Jackie slowly opened the door. She could see and hear nothing.

* * *

It appeared almost out of nowhere. He was working in the bed when he saw it among the Snow in the Mountain. The snake coiled up sunning itself on one of the leaves was only a foot long in length. He did not know if it was poisonous. It simply peered up at him with its beady little eyes. Both creatures eyed each other intently. As if they were sizing each other up like two prize fighters before a match. He could feel the temptation well up inside him. Its gravitational pull drawing him in. The air around him heavy, almost suffocating. He struggled to catch his breath. Suddenly, as quickly as it appeared the snake vanished like a house in the midst of a tornado. It was there one minute then it was gone. But his nerves were still shaken, and the rest of the day was forever changed.

* * *

June 12, 2012

Dear Diary,

Today may be the most miserable day of my life. The school day started with a test in Mr. Noel's science class which I forgot to study for. During Lunch Brad asked Angel to the dance tonight. I pleaded with Mom to buy me a dress but since there were no adults present at the dance Mom said I couldn't go. I am so angry with her lately. Like she totally does not understand me. All she wants me to do is stay at home and be with her all the time. Like doesn't she understand that I have my own life to live? I told her that now I knew why dad left us that she is too controlling for anyone to stand. Tonight, I am staying over at Taylor's house. Taylor's always been my best friend. She and I are practically sisters. Besides she might have a plan for getting us to the party tonight.

* * *

It could be something or it could be nothing. Lee watched as a teal colored Ford Taurus made its way to one of the stalls at the gas station. There was something odd about the vehicle. The paint on the back part just above the fender was peeling. There was nothing odd about this except the way in which the paint was peeling off struck him as strange. The pattern was inconsistent with normal wear and tear. It started in the center above the fender then branched out back towards the front of the vehicle. It reminded Lee of the markings made on his hummer after the blast. This vehicle could have been in some type of explosion.

There was a man in the driver's seat who seemed anxious. He constantly peered into his rearview mirror before getting out of the vehicle and going inside. Lee used this opportunity to inspect the vehicle more closely. The tires looked worn, and the muffler was loose. Lee took out his pocket knife and scrapped some of the paint and rust off of the area that was scorched. The lab could tell him whether or not there was any bomb residue.

* * *

He was finishing his chores in the back yard. Suddenly, he noticed it. The bugs had hit it hard this year, and the leaves were starting to curl and fall one by one to the ground. The one lonely lilac bush in the corner by the fence. Maybe it was the moment itself, but the sun seemed to zero in on this bush and even in its depleted state it glowed with life. He knew it would continue to glow until the last of those leaves fell to the ground. Until the winter of its soul came and the plant was no more but a skeleton in the landscape. Aren't we all depleted souls heading for our own reckoning? The seasons come and go and we remain but for a little while longer on this earth to let a drop of our life force trickle down our souls and kiss the cold hard earth. We sprout flowers or weeds in our wake depending on these legacies. How will we be remembered in the final analysis of our lives? What footprints will we leave in the sand? A clichéd thought that never seems to go away. It can forever haunt us in our dreams for the future.

* * *

He was nearing the end of the sermon much to the relief of his congregation. "Where is the hope? Where is the hope? The hope dear Christian is found in the life, death, burial, and resurrection of the Lord Jesus Christ. The prophet Isaiah prophesized this when he wrote in Isaiah 9:2-7, "The people who walked in darkness have seen a great light; those who dwelt in a land of deep darkness, on them has light shone. You have multiplied the nation; you have increased its joy; they rejoice before you as with joy at the harvest, as they are glad when they divide the spoil. For the yoke of his burden, and the staff for his shoulder, the rod of his oppressor, you have broken as on the day of Midian. For every boot of the tramping warrior in battle tumult and every garment rolled in blood will be burned as fuel for the fire.

For to us a child is born, to us a son is given; and the government shall be upon his shoulder, and his name shall be called Wonderful Counselor, Mighty God, Everlasting Father, Prince of Peace.

Of the increase of his government and of peace there will be no end, on the throne of David and over his kingdom, to establish it and to uphold it with justice and with righteousness from this time forth and forevermore. The zeal of the LORD of hosts will do this.' There is no other way to the Father but through the blood of Jesus. Any other way you travel is the way to destruction."

* * *

It felt petty what she was doing, and she knew it to be wrong but that urge to strike out on her own compelled her to act. With a burrowed dress from Taylor and a ride from her older brother, both girls put the thought of their indiscretion out of their minds and focused on the party.

Katiyln Timms was hosting. Her parents off vacationing in the Caribbean. The Timms had a large rock patio off their house with an infinity pool in the center. Tikki torches lit up the backyard and patio area. When the girls arrived a keg had already been cracked and martinis were being made in the kitchen. Sam felt a little uneasy at the sight of so much alcohol, but she accepted a glass when it was offered to her. After all it would be alright. She finally felt that she was in control of her own life. She gave little thought to the consequences of her actions.

* * *

A feeling of acute trepidation came over him since the night of the blast. Every car door that was shut, every voice that he heard was either the police or the *Vigiles* coming to get him. Jarvis was wondering what the others were doing now as he peered out from the window of his apartment. Night had fallen. He watched as the lights from the passing motorists moved past him on the street. He needed to relax, but in order to relax he needed something to release his body from all this stress. He grabbed his jacket and locked the door to the apartment. He made his way down St. John's before turning left on to 32nd. He was anxious and nervous and he walked faster than he normally did. As if some unseen monster was slowly stalking him. He constantly looked over his shoulder.

CHAPTER 4

L ee slowly scraped his knife across the bottom part of the window.
The latch gave way and he eased himself into the room. The
apartment belonged to a Jarvis Green who Cace said owned the teal
colored Ford Taurus. The lab was still analyzing the paint chips, but
Lee wanted to see who this Jarvis Green really was. If that was even
his name. Of course anything he found in the apartment would never
stand up in court, but he needed to see when the next shipment was
going down.

The apartment was almost bare except for a few pieces of furniture,
a TV, and a frig. On the kitchen table there was a stack of engineering
magazines and some mail that was opened. Lee carefully thumbed
through it all. He then made his way into the bedroom. He found a 12
gauge shot gun and a .308 hunting rifle between the mattresses. There
was a biography on the Weathermen on the night stand. Lee thumbed
through the pages. He was just about to put the biography back on the
night stand when a piece of paper fell out of the binding. Lee picked it
up to examine it. There was a long number written hastily in black ink.

33 47 98 12 48

Lee wasn't sure what the numbers stood for, but he carefully put
the piece of paper back into the book and left the apartment.

He was just climbing back into his truck when he heard it on the
police scanner.

"All units be advised. Shots fired at King's Apartment Complex. Apartment number 452. Repeat 452."

It was Jackie's apartment.

* * *

Her mouth was dry. Her breath labored as she lay on the floor. Mark's hand was clutching a towel around her stomach. The .380 pistol lay on the ground beside her. She had fired three shots into the man as he came through the front door. Unfortunately, he had gotten off a shot of his own. The man was now lying dead by the front door. Jackie knew that the police were coming because she could hear the sirens wailing outside. She just needed to hold on a little while longer. The room around her seemed to spin as she struggled to remain conscious.

* * *

Like the bell high a top McMullen Hall that rings every hour, the sirens wailed past his bedroom window every night. The piercing cries of shattered dreams met with the piercing sounds of progress. Billings the city of a few was set to become the city of many. Stores and restaurants sprung up on every corner. Large banks appeared almost overnight. People packed the movie theaters, studio theaters, and the Metra Park every weekend.

* * *

This was going to be his final remark, and he hoped that they were listening. "Because Jesus is the only way to salvation does it not mean that God is sovereign over all things? In Hebrews 11:3 the author writes, 'By faith we understand that the universe was created by the word of God, so that what is seen was not made out of things that are visible.'" And we see this again in Matthew 6: 9-13 when Jesus is teaching his disciples how to pray. He tells them "Pray then like this: 'Our Father in heaven, hallowed be your name. Your kingdom come, your will be done, on earth as it is in heaven. Give us this day our daily bread, and forgive us our debts, as we also have forgiven our debtors. And lead us not into temptation, but deliver us from evil.'"

* * *

The room and the people in that room were blurred together so that one could not distinguish one from the other. Sometime during the night she had made her way from the room and out on to the patio. She looked up to the dark sky above her for relief for the lights from passing motorists were too much for her eyes. She would go home. She was wrong, that much she knew. Her actions all seemed ridiculous now. She stumbled from the patio on to the street. She found that if she focused on the dark sky over head she could walk a straighter line on the sidewalk.

He noticed her when he rounded the corner and stopped. Jarvis knew by the way she was walking that she was drunk. He eyed the beauty of her figure against the moonlight. She looked to be 16. Her hair dark and long. The dress that she wore was white with red flowers covering every inch of the fabric. She was almost upon him when he realized his chance. There was an alley off to the left, and he grabbed her hand and pulled her over to some garbage cans. He threw her to the ground.

* * *

He had dreamed the dream before, but it disturbed him now more than ever before. It all seemed so real to him so vivid. He remembered walking along a deserted road. He could smell nothing but sweat emanating from his body. His mouth was dry, and his lips were parched by an afternoon sun. The flimsiness of his legs, his cramping muscles, and heavy breathing made him feel like he had been walking a long time.

He tried to move his arms, but his shoulders felt like a ton of bricks. Rest is what he needed, but something inside of him told him to keep moving.

Suddenly, something vibrated in his pocket. Some strange device he did not know he possessed. He fished his right hand into his left jacket pocket. He could feel something solid and smooth touching his fingers, pulling the object out he discovered a cell phone. But it wasn't his cell phone. How did it get there? Did he pick it up by mistake as he was leaving work? He did not know. Trying to wet his lips with what little saliva he had left he answered the phone.

"Hello?"

"Having a nice stroll in the sun are we?" A strong male voice sneered on the other end.

"Who is this?" he asked. "And how do you know I'm outside."

"I know a lot of things about you."

"Who are you?"

"Let's say, it's someone you should know but probably don't." The male voice seemed to be chuckling at the other end.

"Please help me." He found it difficult to speak. His throat was dryer than he had previously realized.

"It's amusing to hear the cries of help echoing from those who never give it." The male voice answered.

"Perhaps I would be inclined to help you if you answered one very simple question for me."

"Two roads diverged in a yellow wood, / And sorry I could not travel both/ And be one traveler, long I stood/ And looked down one as far as I could/ To where it bent in the undergrowth; Two roads one choice which did I chose?"

"Look I'm sorry but I don't know the answer."

"Then I am sorry too." The stranger replied.

"I'm sorry that the bomb strapped to your back will detonate in 4 hours. I wouldn't stop walking if I was you either. The device is motion activated. You stop walking and it detonates."

Sweat dripped from his forehead at a much more rapid pace. He looked feverishly all around him. There existed no farm houses, no gas stations, no buildings of any kind where he might be able to call for help. He was alone.

"And I wouldn't think of calling for help." The stranger added as if reading his thoughts.

"Because if you do I'll drop you right where you stand."

The stranger must have a rifle on him he reasoned. But where could a potential killer be hiding? There was a set of rolling hills and cornfields to his left, but the hills were at least 800 yards away. Too far for any experienced marksman. However, what other cover existed? There was nothing to his right except dry, barren wheat fields, nothing right in front of him except the silent lonely road. That left the hills or whatever lay behind him which couldn't be much.

No. He thought the stranger must be in those hills. Somewhere. He wished he could wake up from this nightmare.

Suddenly, he could hear the faint crunching noise of someone walking through the tall corn stalks to his left.

"How's it feel to see your life hang in the balance?" He could hear the stranger sneering again on the other end.

"What do you want from me?" He managed to ask after a while.

"I want you to go on a journey with me to hell."

For the first two hours, it was more or less the same routine. The stranger would tell him either to go left, or right, take this gravel road, or stay on the secondary road.

He was shocked, for the world around him seemed dead. Out of those two hours no one drove past him.

Suddenly, he could hear something rumbling behind him. It must be a car. Perhaps he could motion to the driver that he was in danger, but as fast as this small measure of hope entered his mind an even bigger fear became apparent. What if the stranger turned his sights on his would be rescuer? He would be responsible for that person's death. Even if he made it out of this ordeal, he would have to live with the knowledge that he killed another human being.

Oddly, he prayed that the stranger would just drive past him. Disregard him as maybe a lost tourist out on a little summer walk, not a 30 year old local with a pack of explosives strapped to his back.

The vehicle was almost upon him now, the driver slowing down. God help me. He thought dropping the phone. One thing was for certain he could not stop walking. If he stopped he would blow both of them up.

"Give me the pack." He could hear the driver of the vehicle say to him.

"I don't know how." He heard himself say.

"Yes you do." He could hear the driver reply. "Just trust me."

Suddenly the vehicle was gone.

The report of the rifle made him jump. He could see where the stranger's shot had caused an indentation to form in the ground in front of him. Another shot rang out, and another indention formed in the ground in front of him. Except this one was a little further out than the previous one. After a couple more shots, he realized that the stranger was leading him towards something. Following the direction of the shots he saw the cell phone the stranger used to talk to him sitting in the gravel.

Picking up the phone he put it to his ear.

"Hello?"

"Turn around." The stranger replied.

He slowly turned around. A shot rang out hitting him in his left foot. Crying out he instinctively tried to grab his foot in an attempt to stop the bleeding; however, not wanting to drop the phone again he kept his right hand holding the phone and shifted his weight to his right foot. The pain was horrendous.

"You think still your smarter than me!" The stranger hollered into the phone.

"How much farther do we have to go?" He asked through the pain.

"You have only two hours left so not long." The stranger replied.

He had not been keeping track of the time during the whole exchange with the deputy, but now it seemed as if an invisible clock rested on his back. Every second that passed hurdle him that much closer to his fate of dying at the hands of this monster.

"Ready for another test?"

He heaved a big sigh. "Yes."

"Good, because there is an intersection coming up. A place where two roads branch out from the main. I want you to choose one, only one."

"If you choose the right one. Then you will be that much closer to coming out of this ordeal alive."

"And if I choose the wrong road?" He asked.

"It will be the last choice you ever have to make."

Suddenly, two roads besides the one he was walking on appeared before him. One was a typical gravel road much like the one he had been traveling on for most of the day. The other didn't really resemble a road at all but instead looked like two ditches running side by side each other. Than it dawned on him that the ditches were not ditches at all, but tire ruts long over grown with weeds and wild snake grass. He was sure this was the road. "I took the one less traveled by/ And that has made all the difference."

This road was obviously the lesser traveled of the two. What if he was wrong though? What if his captor meant to kill him regardless of the road he took? This road was probably better for a murder anyway, but he had to choose. It wasn't like he could stand and contemplate which one. He was fast approaching the cutoff that lead to the road he wanted, five to six feet from him. He needed to make a decision.

He decided to take a chance, a leap of faith if one could call it that into the shadowy undergrowth that surrounded the old road.

Hobbling for about a hundred yards he rounded a bend in the road and could make out the rusted frame of a Ford pick-up. It was smashed against a large old cotton tree and from what he could see it appeared the driver must have over corrected from the gravel road, and crashed down here.

"It's quite a crash isn't?" The stranger asked.

"Yes it is." He said almost in a whisper.

He knew death was close by, he could almost feel its breath on the hairs of his neck. He thought desperately about what to do. There could only be about 15 minutes left on the bomb. If only he could find a way to disarm it, but he knew nothing about bombs. He desperately wanted to wake up from this dream.

He whipped the sweat from his palms. His right hand brushing against something. A wire perhaps. He brought his right hand down again. Sure enough. He could feel two wires roll across his fingertips.

What if he cut one of them? Would that disarm the bomb? What could he use to cut it with? His eyes frantically searched the ground for a scrape of metal or a piece of broken glass. Finally, his eyes caught the reflection of something shining sitting in the grass.

He pretended to trip just as his right hand touched the ground to break his fall. The piece of glass clinched tightly in his hand as he quickly got up.

But even if he diffused the bomb, how was he going to escape the shooter's deadly aim? Suddenly, an idea took root, a last ditch effort of hope entered his mind.

He winced at the pain as the glass began to cut through the wire and his flesh.

He held his breath as he felt the wire began to give. This is it he thought, moment of truth.

He kept hobbling so as not to let the stranger know what he had done.

He knew the stranger was about to pull the trigger. There existed a certain finality to his voice. A certain end to his anger and pain. Suddenly, instead of hearing the report of the rifle all he could hear was a click on the other end of the phone. A misfire. Not waiting for the stranger to reload he dropped to his knees, and in one swift motion slipped the backpack from his shoulders. Rolling away from it he could hear a whizzing noise as a bullet ricocheted off a tree in front of him. The stranger's second shot.

By then he was off in an all out hobbled sprint for freedom. His arms pumping just as fast as his legs. Navigating through a pile of dense underbrush he began to climb in evaluation. Finally, he crested a small hill. The bright afternoon sun beat heavily on his face.

He searched frantically for help. Anybody or anything that could render him assistance. Nothing though lay before him except vast empty acres of farmland. Suddenly, a twig snapped behind him, but he did not look back. Quickly descending the small hill he found himself on a gravel road. No doubt the same road he had previously been traveling on.

However, not wanting to make too fine of target for his pursuer he chose instead to cross the road and enter into some more dense underbrush. Twigs snapped and scratched across his face until small gashes formed that began to bleed. He couldn't hear anything behind him.

Crossing through an area where the brush was surprisingly light, he stopped abruptly in his tracks.

An old homestead lay about five hundred yards in front of him. The roof was partially caved in and from what he could tell from the rusted farm equipment scattered about, nobody really knew or cared if this place existed.

Half-walking, half-jogging the two hundred yards of terrain that lay between him and the homestead, he could see a small out building directly behind the actual house. It was too large to be an outhouse, a tool shed maybe.

He slowly opened the door. The hinges creaked something fierce as he peered inside.

Numerous tools lay strung about. Hammers, shovels, and rusted saw blades, but one tool caught his attention. A rusted sledge hammer, but this sledge hammer was in the shape of a cross.

He listened closely to the wind as it gently blew across the trees. He thought he heard something. A faint crunching noise that a pair of boots make on uneven ground. He situated himself behind the tool shed and waited.

The crunching noise got louder. The stranger couldn't be no more than 300 yards from the homestead he thought. He looked down at the pick and wondered if he had the nerve to kill. It was a matter of survival wasn't it? Him or the stranger. Only one was going to walk out of this place still breathing. He gripped the sledge hammer tighter as the crunching noise came closer. That person was going to be him. The crunching noise was maybe about four feet from the shed. He could hear the stranger's heavy breathing. How had the man known he was behind the shed? It was like he had tracked him the same way a predator tracks his prey.

He guessed the man was about five feet away from him. He would have to swing the sledge wide.

The tension mounted to a nerve racking crescendo. Somehow the stranger knew what he was thinking. No. He thought. I'm letting my imagination get away from me.

Frost's words came back to him now. "And be one traveler, long I stood"

His hands almost stark white and covered in blood gripped the sledge handle harder. Suddenly, taking a deep breath he swung the sledge with all his might as he advanced from the back of the tool shed. The sledge hit its target, just above the stranger's groin. He could hear the man as he cried cry out in agony. At the same time the stranger dropped the rifle that was in his hands. The weapon discharged. The bullet hitting a pile of rocks behind the two men.

He didn't wait for the stranger to make the next move. Tackling the man to the ground he used his good leg put as much weight on the stranger's chest as he could. Doubling up his fists he started to beat the man's face. It was as if he suddenly possessed the spirit of some wild animal. He only stopped when he lost all feeling in his hands. Taking a deep breath, he looked down at the stranger's bloody face, and only then realized that the man was not breathing. It was then that he realized that the man lying before him was himself. He then woke up from the dream unsettled by it all.

CHAPTER 5

The air around the waiting room seemed thick and stifling hot. Micah sweated profusely under his suit jacket. He took a deep breath to calm himself down. His wife was going to have a baby. He was going to be a father. My what joy God brings to those who wait on him, he thought. The church he worked at was growing. Slowly mind you but growing and now a baby. The joy in his heart was overwhelming. But would he be a good father? He begin to take notice of the rest of the people in the waiting room with him. One was a portly old gentleman in a Christmas sweater and khakis who was thumbing his way through a copy of Sports Illustrated. A woman was sitting a couple seats down from him texting on her smartphone while apparently listening to music. The next was a man who appeared to be about Micah's age. The man wore a buttoned up flannel shirt, blue jeans, and black, steel toed work boots. The man seemed to be racked in the torrents of grief. He was hunched over. His face buried in his hands. The phone beside him kept vibrating, but the man refused to answer it. Micah suddenly felt his heart go out to this man, and he walked over to where the man was sitting.

"What troubles you sir?"

"That I might lose again the things that were taken from me when I was young."

"What things would that be?" Micah asked.

"A sister who was shot tonight and a niece who was raped."

Micah was not sure how to respond and just stared at the man.

"Where is God in all this suffering? Where is God in all this chaos? How can a loving God let such evil walk the face of the earth?"

Micah prayed a silent pray before he respond to the man's questions. The question is how a loving God can allow sinners like us to live and not destroy us. The answer is Grace. "Before creation began God predestined or decided who was going to be saved and live with him in eternity in heaven and who was going to be condemned and spend an eternity in hell. Meaning that there are some people who walk the face of the earth in open rebellion to God and some who walk the earth in harmony with God because they have repented of their sins and believe in Jesus Christ. They have received Christ's imputed righteousness through the process of justification and now live their lives through the constant cleansing of their sins through the process of sanctification. That is why there is evil walking this earth. God has chosen to do this though so in the end he is glorified. God raised up Pharaoh in the bible to show to the Israelites that he is a loving and just God. He showed this by annihilating Pharaoh's army and protecting the Israelites as they left Egypt. All of those who love, honor, and follow Christ never are alone in the world as dark as it is."

"I have fought through the darkness my whole life. It has hounded me every step of the way."

"What's your name?" Micah asked.

"Lee." The man answered.

"Well Lee in Psalm 23:4-6 David writes, 'Even though I walk through the valley of the shadow of death, I will fear no evil, for you are with me; your rod and your staff, they comfort me. You prepare a table before me in the presence of my enemies; you anoint my head with oil; my cup overflows. Surely goodness and mercy shall follow me all the days of my life, and I shall dwell in the house of the Lord forever.' Meaning that if we repent, believe, and follow Christ he will never leave us nor forsake us."

* * *

The grief of the situation subsided and an angry rage soon took its place. He still intended to fulfill his mission to find out about the shipment of guns and dismantle the organization, but he was going to start handling things differently. The gloves were off. The darkness that he had been fighting his whole life was affecting a family he hardly knew. But they were still his family, and he needed to start looking out for them.

He paused by his sister's room before leaving the hospital. The nurse after much prodding said she was in critical condition. She had lost a lot of blood and the next 24 hours would determine whether she lived or died. He looked through the window into the room. She lying there motionless on the bed. Tubes seemed to be sticking out all over her body. Lee remembered when he and Jackie were kids and how they used to share a bed in the small two bedroom apartment they shared with their step parents.

"Lee did you see that?" Jackie would ask some nights.

"See what?"

"It looks like a monster."

"Jackie go back to sleep." Lee would always say trying to go back to sleep himself.

"It's coming closer. It's eyes are glaring back at me. Lee I'm scared."

Lee would feel Jackie shivering under the covers. He tried to reassure her.

"Monsters don't exist Jackie and even if they did being afraid of them won't make them go away." He had said.

"But I don't know how to stop being afraid." Jackie would say.

"I don't know how to be brave."

Those words seemed to haunt him now as he watched his sister fighting for her life on a hospital bed. He found himself saying a silent prayer for her and his niece who was still being examined and treated. He prayed to a god he barely knew. He did not know what else to do.

Lee did not know what was out there. He had long pondered it, but the answer always seemed to elude him. Perhaps he was eluding it. Sometimes he dreamt that he was all alone in a large wooded area. Something would rustle in the bushes to his right. He would walk towards the noise, but before he could peer into the brush something deep within his soul would force him to shriek in terror and run away without knowing what was in that bush.

"Run to the father. He will protect you." The preacher had said.

"Cry out to God for even in your darkest misery he is there."

"He will lay down your torch and show you the way through his son Jesus Christ."

Evil is the pervasion of will. Vigilantism is the slippery slope of anarchy. When man starts playing god it is his children that suffer. If that's the case we must all be a world of orphans by now. Lee thought. Did that mean that God didn't exist? He knew little of the supernatural. He had blood on his hands that was all he knew. If there was a God that could make that blood disappear he must be a magician. Lee reasoned as he turned on to the street where Jarvis lived.

His phone had been vibrating all night and he knew it was Cace. He had not reported in yet, and he knew Cace would be concerned. But he had to talk to Jarvis face to face even if it meant exposing his own cover.

* * *

For the first time in the last couple of days he felt relaxed. His mind was at ease. He was just making his way through the front door of the apartment when suddenly a hand grabbed him by his coat collar and pulled him inside. He could not see who the attacker was maybe some street thug looking for dope money. He was just about to call out for help when he felt the sharp pain of a man's fist slam into his face. He was momentarily knocked unconscious. When he finally came to he noticed that he was strapped to a chair, and his attacker was sitting barely two feet across from him. Only he could not see the man's face because he was wearing a ski mask that had holes cut out for the man's eyes and mouth. The man spoke.

"We're going to play a little game. I ask questions. You give me answers. If you don't give me answers that I want I put a bullet in your foot, then your kneecap, then your arms, and finally your head. Understand?"

Jarvis nodded his head. The man began.

"What is the number 33 mean?"

"If I tell you that I am dead anyway." Jarvis answered.

A load blast suddenly filled the room, and Jarvis cried out though the bullet entered the floor in front of them.

"33?" The man asked again.

"Number of guns." Jarvis said trying to control himself.

"47?" The man asked.

"I don't know." Jarvis said.

A second shot rang out.

"AK 47s!" He cried out in fear.

"And the last three numbers?" The man asked.

"They are coordinates." Jarvis said trying to keep focused.

"Coordinates to what?" The man hollered.

"A grave in a cemetery." Jarvis said.

Lee had heard enough. There were not that many cemeteries in the city with those coordinates. He could find the spot and wait for the groups to make the exchange. First though he needed to contact Cace. His phone vibrated again. Flipping it open he read Cace's message. He wanted to meet at an old warehouse on the south side of town. He gave Lee the address.

CHAPTER 6

Approaching the building from the south, Lee slowly and deliberately made his way to the entrance on the east side of the building where Cace was standing and pacing nervously.

"You should have told me about the sister. Lee this case is already in the crapper without you bringing your personal life into it."

"You would have taken me off the case." Lee shot back.

"You're right, I would have taken you off the case." Cace said.

"What do you mean this case is in the crapper?" Lee asked.

"The government does not want the ATF or the FBI involved in this case anymore."

"What?" Lee asked.

"The state department does not feel that the threat is deadly enough to warrant our attention."

"They're blowing people up Cace."

"I don't know for sure at this point, but based off of what we know about this vigilante group I would say we are dealing with something a lot more lethal than a few law abiding citizens."

"In the government's eyes that's all we're dealing with." Cace said. "Wake up Lee. They were never going to go through with this case. The only reason this thing even got started was because they knew that they needed to show the world that they are tough on terrorism and illegal gun trafficking. The bottom line is these guys are doing the agency's dirty work for them."

"So this is what its come down to. The federal government relying on a group of mercenaries."

"Think about it. The government has a force of law abiding citizens that it can set loose on the general population. This group is bound by no laws, cost little to maintain, and if they go too far in killing bad guys the government simply washes its hands of them and pretends that it didn't know."

"That's the practical side of politics." Cace said relighting his cigar.

"Tomorrow morning we pull out of here, and the day after they want our reports turned in." Cace said walking back to his car which Lee could see was parked a hundred yards away behind a pile of scrap metal. Lee watched as his friend went to open the car door. Suddenly, a loud explosion erupted in front of him knocking Lee backwards. He landed on his back in a daze. It took him a couple of seconds to realize that the explosion came from Cace's car. Looking up he could see the car burning in a great ball of fire.

Taking his pistol up in his hand, Lee bolted over a concrete barrier and began running down the sidewalk in the direction of the truck.

His heart was racing as he rounded the corner. Two dark figures were racing towards him from the opposite side of the street. Without thinking Lee leveled the pistol and from a crouching position and opened fire. The two figures dropped dead in the middle of the street. Another figure was approaching the truck from behind. Lee saw him in the corner of his eye and spun around to open fire, but the figure already had his weapon pointed at Lee which Lee could see was a shotgun. He could hear the loud blast of the shotgun and feel the burn of the buckshot as it tore a hole into his left shoulder knocking him sideways. Lee raising his right arm emptied his magazine into the figure and watched as the man dropped onto the sidewalk. He ran over to the man and searched his pockets for identification. The man had none. Lee could hear sirens approaching and without thinking he grabbed each of the men and dumped their bodies in a nearby dumpster.

Lee climbed into the front seat. The pain in his left shoulder throbbed something fierce as he started the truck up and put it in gear all with his right hand. Turning left down 1st Ave. North, Lee weaved his way in and out of traffic all the while keeping a wary eye on who was behind him. He did not notice anything out of the ordinary, until he got past the intersection at 29th street. It was then that he noticed two black SUV's coming up fast behind him.

The first SUV was rapidly approaching him as he made his way through the intersection at North 32nd street. The vehicle slowly pulled up alongside him, and Lee could see a man in a red cape. They are going to try and run me off the road. He thought. Without thinking Lee suddenly turned the truck into the SUV. He did the action so abruptly that he caught the man completely off guard. The man cried out as the driver of the SUV lost control of the vehicle. The vehicle hit the corner of a parked car before it rolled twice through the next intersection.

Lee looked into his rearview mirror and could see the second SUV barreling towards him. Driving through the intersection off of Division, Lee blew past two cars just making their way onto Broadwater. The sound of horns honking pierced the night air, and Lee could hear the deathly crunch as one of the cars plowed into a street lamp. The SUV was still trailing him and gaining ground. Until suddenly, Lee felt the truck lurch forward as the SUV plowed into the back of it. Lee struggled to keep the vehicle on the street. Then Lee watched as the SUV swerved into the middle lane and slowly crept up alongside him. Lee instinctively rolled down his window and holding the stirring wheel with one hand aimed his pistol at the SUV's front left tire and opened fire. At the same time Lee put his foot on the brake pedal and watched as the SUV spun around to its left before rolling twice and landing upside down in the middle of the street. In the same moment, Lee could hear the deathly crunch and shattering of glass as a small passenger van plowed into the back of him. Horns and screeching tire noises were all around them as passersby were trying to avoid the wreck. Lee without stopping gave the truck a little gas and made his way pass the upside down SUV and proceeded down Broadwater until he made a left down 17th. Following the street until he came to Central, he turned down a side road into the old Mountview Cemetery. They should be here soon he thought driving deep into the cemetery before parking behind the caretaker's shop.

Section 98 in the cemetery was 50 yards to his left. He sat in the truck with the lights off waiting. He had been there for an hour and still no one had showed up. In the meantime, Lee got the first-aid kit from the glove compartment and went to work on his left shoulder. It was a painstakingly slow process, and there was a couple of times he very nearly passed out. When he was finished, he cleaned the area again and put a bandage over it.

It was then that he saw movement to his left. It was so dark it was difficult to see, but he could just barely make out the outline of a person standing by a headstone. The figure appeared to be just standing not doing anything else. Then Lee saw a second figure moving across a group of headstones to his right. The figure was carrying something. Lee wasn't sure what. That's when he saw it. A large pickup truck slowly creeping down the road that ran past the headstones. The vehicle got to where the two figures were then stopped.

Lee loaded a fresh magazine into his gun before slowly and quietly making his way out of his vehicle. He skirted the caretaker's garage from the west. He rounded the corner and then sprinted 30 feet across the road before ending up behind a large sarcophagus that stood high above the ground. He peered over the top of the rock and could see the truck 20 yards away in front of him. The driver was out of the vehicle helping the other two men carry a large box from one of the headstones to the truck. Lee realized this was probably his best chance. He reached into his pocket and pulled out his flashlight. With his flashlight in his left hand and his pistol in his right he sprinted towards the truck. He waited until he was right on top of the three men before snapping on his flashlight. His first shot hit the man to his left dead center into the man's chest causing him to drop his portion of the box. The two other men dropped the box and looked towards Lee's direction. Lee stopped and took careful aim with his next two shots. Both bullets found their mark and the men fell to the ground.

When Lee got to the box he noticed the U.S. Army insignia on the side. Breaking the lock he found 33 AK-47s nestled in some packing.

Lee acted fast. Going into the caretaker's garage he found the keys to a skid steer and brought the machine over to the box of rifles. Detaching the bucket from the skid steer he put all the rifles into the bucket along with an old tarp he found. He then carefully dumped a gallon of diesel fuel over the weapons before lighting it all on fire. He then searched the bodies of the dead men. He needed to know where this shipment was heading. He checked all three of the men's cellphones. Each had the same message:

Indian Artwork Shipment

It only took Lee a couple seconds to realize what this meant. Hiding the bodies in the shallow grave that was just dug, Lee jumped into the large pickup and left the cemetery. The rifles were still burning when he left.

CHAPTER 7

At first when she woke up she thought she had been dreaming that the events of the day had not occurred. She was merely at home in bed. But there was something missing. The feeling seemed to pierce her skin into her bones and burrow itself deep within her soul. She felt shattered and alone. She wished her mother was here right now holding her hand, but they had told her no because her mother had been shot and was in the hospital. The pain felt worse after they told her that.

She sat up in the hospital bed. Her feet swung over the side and lightly touched the cold hard tile floor. A nurse came in and told her that she was going home. When she asked how, the nurse answered that a relative, her uncle, had come to take her home. What uncle? She did not even know her mother had a sibling. She felt the loneness surround her as she got dressed.

* * *

Lee left the truck with the empty box parked a little ways down the road from the Pictograph Cave State Park. He grabbed a GPS he found in the cab along with a small computer. When he doubled back to the park itself, he could see the group that was assembled. Some were in black hoods others in red chanting something. The majority of them were huddled around a large bon fire cradling their rifles talking. They would eventually find the truck, but not before Lee figured out who killed Cace.

The explosion ran through his head. Cace was dead. He was certain of that. But why? Did the *Vigiles* know that he was there? If they did why did they wait so long to kill him? Why didn't they kill him that night at the ritual? Unless they felt that he knew nothing to begin with and would be kept on a tight leash by the agency. What if the *Vigiles* had an informant inside the agency itself? That would explain why he was not killed right away. The informant thought Lee would never be able to ID a witness to the first explosion or furthermore make that witness talk about where the shipment was. The informant would have to have known that Cace was going to meet Lee at the warehouse tonight, so whoever Cace talked to before meeting up with Lee could be that informant.

Lee needed to revisit the warehouse to see if he could find any clues that weren't already swept up by the police. He needed to work fast.

The smell of gasoline and burnt flesh still permeated the atmosphere of the blast site. Morning was starting to break, so Lee knew he did not have much time. He walked the perimeter of the blast hoping to get lucky and find Cace's cellphone. The phone could have been destroyed in the explosion or it could have been dropped. He started at the car which was still smoldering and then worked backwards. He scanned the area frantically with his flashlight. The sun hadn't risen enough to be much use in the shadows cast by the warehouse. Suddenly, he caught the reflection of the screen with his light. The phone was a little beat up but amazingly still intact. Lee checked the calls received from the time leading up to the blast. There was an unknown cell number that called Cace minutes before his death but whose number was it. He took out the small laptop he had found in the truck. The laptop was used to track gun shipments coming into and leaving the state. The number of emails detailing business transactions was alarming. Hundreds were made in the last week alone. Some shipments were bigger than others but all looked like they were coming out of Fort Bragg. Apparently, the *Vigiles* had someone helping them on the inside.

He logged on to the bureau's network and ran the cellphone number. It took only about a minute before a name came up. Lincoln Worthington. Lee was puzzled. Apparently, Worthington was a CIA operative with ties to the Middle East. But why would Worthington be calling Cace? Worthington must be the informant. Worthington's file said that he had worked in the Middle East primarily in Afghanistan from 2004-2012 before the agency listed him as missing and off the reservation. What if Worthington was a contact man for the *Vigiles* and the group was using him to smuggle guns out of Afghanistan to bring them north to Montana. Then a lot more people were going to die before this whole thing was through.

* * *

Darkness surrounded her even though she knew it was morning. She remembered leaving the hospital with a man who said he was her uncle, her sister's brother. They walked to the parking lot before coming to a large white cargo van. Then the man disappeared and before she knew it. Sam found herself being grabbed by two other men. The door to the van opened and she found herself being pushed inside. A hood was placed over her head as the van sped away from the hospital.

* * *

Micah had just finished making his rounds at the hospital before coming back to the church. There were a number of people in his congregation with family members sick in the hospital, and he needed to visit and pray with each family. He was exhausted even though it was barely noon. There were storm clouds outside that he noticed when he drove up. The wind was picking up as well.

He was just about to walk through the door when a man stopped him outside. The man was in a panic. A look of fear stretched across his face.

"Can I help you?" Micah asked.

"Yes, there's a man chasing me. He's wearing a red hood and he is tall. O' please help me."

This man was delirious and worse Micah noticed a pool of blood that ran from under the man's pant leg.

Micah helped the man inside and rested him on a pew.

"I'll call the paramedics." Micah assured the man.

"No don't do that."

"Why?" Micah asked perplexed.

"Because he's after them too." The man said before blacking out.

Micah did not know what to do. The storm outside was getting worse, so he kneeled by the man and prayed.

* * *

Officer Martin drove down the main drag of the Heights before making a left on Hilltop. He was going to a house off of Norse Court. The dispatcher said there was an animal loose in a woman's bushes and that it maybe poisonous.

Officer Martin wasn't sure what he was dealing with. Animal Control had been contacted and was en route. Another officer was already on the scene. He took a deep breath as he turned down Nutter Blvd. It had been a year since he was back from Afghanistan and adjusting to civilian life was still taking its toll on him. There were nights he would wake up in a cold sweat and believe he was in an Al-Qaida ambush. That feeling of eyes watching him and that thought that any moment an RPG was about to go off still haunted him. He felt those eyes watching him now but dismissed it as post-traumatic stress. He turned into the driveway and got out of the car. Officer Bane was talking with the woman who seemed pretty upset.

"I don't know where it came from. I was taking out my trash and there it was."

Martin got out his flashlight. There was a small flower bed by the garbage can. A dense row of lilacs was behind it. He began to scan the row of lilacs with his flashlight when suddenly a pair of eyes stared back at him.

"What do we got?" Bane asked joining Martin next to the flower bed.

"Boa constrictor someone's pet."

"Gee can't we wait until winter sets in then he will be begging us to catch him."

"How do you know it's a male?" Martin joked.

"Because a female wouldn't be dumb enough to let herself get pinned down in a row of lilacs."

"Where did you hear that?"

"National Geographic had a special on last night."

"Well do you think you can find me a garbage bag there Ranger Rick." Martin quipped.

"I ain't touching that thing."

"Why? Afraid it might try and sell you car insurance." Martin joked.

"O' we are full of jokes this evening are we?"

Martin couldn't help it. Jokes took the edge off, and he still felt like multiple eyes were watching them.

"Ask her if she's got a garbage bag."

"What's Lewis' excuse for being late to a scene? Animal Control. What is he doing trapping an alligator up by Boothill?" Bane moaned.

The woman went inside to grab a bag. The two men begin to haze the snake out of the bushes when the first shot rang out. It hit Bane. He dropped to the ground motionless.

Martin dropped to the ground and drew his pistol. A shot hit the ground five feet to his right. The shot actually hit the snake, and Martin watched as the wounded animal crawled miserably deeper into the bushes. By this time he had the passenger door open to his squad car and was reaching for his 30.06 he kept on the sit. Another shot ricocheted and hit his right rearview mirror. Bullets were whizzing all around him and he suddenly came to the grim realization that there were multiple shooters. The whole thing smelled like an ambush. Grabbing the rifle he made his way to the front of the patrol car. The bullets were still flying all around him mostly hitting the car when he realized that he was pinned down and wasn't going anywhere for a while.

He eyed the dead body of his fellow officer on the driveway and realized that the war had never left him.

* * *

He was impatient and nervous. He constantly peered out the window watching the traffic pass by him. All those going home commuters bumper to bumper making a mad dash home to their sweethearts and kids. A momentary feeling of regret came over him, but he pushed it away. He might have been able to have that once but not anymore. Benghazi, Istanbul, Kabul, four continents and too many places whose names he could no longer remember. He was 48 years old, and Lincoln Worthington was tired of running. He longed for those simple days out on his father's ranch where all that mattered was livestock. Peace was what he yearned for as he sat alone in his hotel room. But he had to sell his soul to the devil to get it. He smuggled the guns out of Afghanistan for them, and they had rewarded him generously. His flight left in the morning. It was bond for Alaska. Maybe peace would finally find him there. There was a knock on the door. He opened the door. A man in a black hood was in the doorway. The gun was leveled, and the silencer went off. In those fleeting moments, he could see his father's ranch. The horses in the pasture then it was gone.

CHAPTER 8

He had an idea on how to track the *Vigiles*, but he needed to contact his friend at the FBI Teresa Stone. Lee was just about ready to reach for his phone when suddenly the phone begin to vibrate on its own. Lee looked at the number. It was Hermes.

"We have your niece and have been to the hospital where your sister is being held. You either give yourself up or they die bad. Noon tomorrow to comply."

Before Lee could respond Hermes disconnected. He tried desperately to quiet the fear welling up inside him. It took him a couple minutes to calm his nerves before calling Teresa.

The two had met during basic training, had both served a time in Afghanistan, and had both continued their careers in law enforcement after the war. Lee considered Teresa a good friend. He knew of no one else he could trust.

He dialed her number. Got her voicemail. Dialed her number again and finally reached her.

"Look I know this could get you into trouble, but I need you to track a GPS signal and see if any other vehicles have the same GPS signal in my area."

Minutes passed while Teresa worked furiously on the computer.

"Alright there are eight other vehicles emitting the same GPS signal as yours." Teresa said.

"Can you send the information to a lap top computer I have sitting in front of me?"

"It is going to take a little while."

After about an hour, Lee found himself staring at the exact position of the eight vehicles.

"Thanks doll I owe you big time."

"Duly noted. I am putting it on your tab."

Suddenly, Lee noticed two patrol cars zoom past him down the street with their sirens blaring. His gut instinct told him that he should follow them. He followed them down 4th, turned left at the intersection at the Metra before ending up at a large hotel. Lee followed the officers as they made their way through the lobby and up to the 8th floor. They made their way down a narrow hallway before entering a room to the left of the elevator marked 811. Lee needed to get into that room without the police seeing him. He reached over and tripped the fire alarm and waited. Pretty soon the officers ran out of the room and exited via the stairway across from the elevators.

Lee ran into the room and was surprised to see Worthington's body lying on the floor. He knew he only had moments before the police realized the ruse and came back, so he searched the room for anything left by the *Vigiles* or Worthington. In the air duct above the bed, he discovered a small notebook. Inside the notebook were the names and descriptions of each of the places where a weapons exchange had taken place between Worthington and the *Vigiles*. It was interesting that the name of each place was a cemetery. Some of the cemeteries were quite old and seldom used anymore. Who would know where each old cemetery was at? A county official. Why would a county official want to do that? There was a local election coming up perhaps this person wanted to hide his or her dark past in the hopes of getting elected. The drug dealer, and bookstore owner could all have ties to the leader of the *Vigiles*. This person could not only want to clear their dark past but want to use it as political leverage. Lee stuffed the notebook in his pocket and made his way out of the hotel. He was running out of time.

* * *

The view from her office window was a complete view of the city. It was from here that she could see Sacrifice Cliff where the Indians ran the buffalo off. She could see the two major refineries chugging out products from their smelters. The trains still came through downtown just right below her. She could see the cars stopped at the crossing and wondered how long the drive home was going to be. A small price to pay for progress but yet she had been paying these small prices her whole life. A ward of the state when she was 10. She was living on the streets by age 16. She meet a wealthy business man who trafficked drugs who agreed to pay her $100,000 if she agreed to be his wife. She pocketed the money and shortly thereafter the man died. She got her law degree from Yale and came back to Billings to run her own private practice. But her past clung to her like the smell left by the streets. The mixture of trash and urine never left her. But then came the election and the promise of a rich donor to clean the slate. She jumped at the opportunity even though she feared being shackled to another man. But he had made good on his promise so far, and as she sat alone in her office that day she felt quietly optimistic.

* * *

He stopped to catch his breath behind an outcropping of sandstone high atop the rims. Day light had come, and Martin had been on the move all night. It had taken him several hours to pin point the location of the shooter but he managed to isolate the sound from the report of the rifle to this area. On the climb up here he had detected a glimmer from a rifle barrel 50 yards to his left. He knew he was getting close because he could hear some movement on the rocks. It may be a small fox or a mountain lion hunting, but it might also be his shooter. He waited and listened.

The sound seemed to be getting closer. He took the safety off his rifle. Suddenly, barely 10 yards from his position he could see a man creeping slowly over the rock. It did not appear that the man was aware of his presence, so Martin lifted the rifle to his shoulder and took careful aim. The sound from his rifle echoed off the rock and he watched as the man dropped his rifle and fell 20ft below him. The hunter had gotten his prey.

* * *

Lee spotted the first vehicle. It was sitting in an alley just off of Montana Ave. Time was short, and he was already exposed, so Lee decided to approach the vehicle from the front with his pistol drawn. The driver was looking to his right and did not know Lee was there until Lee was within 20ft of the vehicle. But by then it was too late. Lee leveled his 45 and emptied the magazine into the windshield of the car. He reloaded and walked slowly up to the driver side window. He could see the man in the driver's seat. He was dead.

Searching the car Lee found a bag of weapons in the back seat. Four pipe bombs, an M-1 rifle, and a 12 gauge shot-gun plus boxes of ammo. Lee lit one of the pipe bombs and stuck it under the hood of the car. He was just about to turn the corner back on to 1st when he heard the explosion. One down seven more to go.

* * *

"A man or woman with sin in their heart and who does not repent is like a wild wounded animal tearing through a vast wilderness of darkness. Nothing but destruction lays in their wake. Fear blinds them to the truth of God's love, and death is the only friend they will find in the end. But there is a hunter who hunts for lost souls. The demons fear him, and Satan himself shakes in dread. And he will find you in the end and restore your heart back to its full potential. Heal old wounds that have become infected over time. He will heal. He will restore. He will breathe new life into your soul." Micah had once said to his congregation.

He had done his best to stop the bleeding, but the man was losing blood fast. Micah had the man stretched out on the floor of the sanctuary. The man was still babbling on about a stranger in a red cape. Micah did not know what to do. He had been praying in earnest for the last four hours asking God for guidance, strength, and wisdom.

He was walking back from the janitor's closet with some fresh towels when he saw the figure the man was talking about. He was tall, a red cape draped over his face obscured his eyes, but Micah could see the stubble from an unshaven face. Suddenly, fear gripped at his heart, and he felt paralyzed by it. He could not move. He just stood there watching this figure of death approach him, and he found himself saying one more silent prayer. A bizarre scene unfolded around him. The man in the red cape was walking down the sidewalk to the church while a homeless old man was walking down the sidewalk from the other direction. When both men saw each other they stopped. They just stood there facing each other than the man in the red cape turned and fled. Then suddenly the homeless man was standing before Micah in the church.

"Do not be afraid help is on the way." The man said and then he was gone. And before Micah could say a word an ambulance came blaring down the street before pulling up to the church.

* * *

Lee approached this vehicle from the Northside of the street. He had already lit the pipe bomb, and he was just about to lob it into the cab when the driver saw him. The man turned and went for his gun. Lee threw the bomb through the driver side window and drew his 45 while at the same time backing away from the truck. The man was just taking aim when the bomb exploded in the cab killing the man instantly.

Lee was just turning to walk away when he heard someone behind him yell.

"Freeze don't move!"

* * *

The man was still babbling on incoherently about the man in the red cape as the ambulance made its way to the hospital. Paramedics found a wallet in his back pocket. Driver's License read Jarvis Green. Micah watched the man convulse in the gurney until the morphine kicked in.

Why God have you put me in this position? Micah thought.

When they got to the hospital the man was rushed into surgery. A police man came up to the waiting room and asked Micah some questions. Apparently the man matched a description given by a young girl earlier who said she had been raped. The officer drove Micah back to headquarters to give his statement and to answer more questions.

When they got to the police station the police were bringing another man in. Micah could see the man's hands handcuffed behind him. Suddenly, he recognized the man from the hospital. He felt his heart go out to this man though he did not know his full story. He just knew that whatever trouble this man caused it was because of the pain he was feeling in his heart.

After giving his statement, he asked if he could see the man.

"Maybe he'll talk to you because he sure doesn't want to talk to us." The officer who brought him said leading Micah to the prisoner's cell.

The man slowly looked up as Micah sat down close to the bars then the man looked down again.

The man began to speak. "Everything I touch shatters into a million pieces. I try to pick up those pieces but every time I try a strong wind comes up and blows them away. I asked God's forgiveness, but I still feel the blood on my hands. As hard as I wash it won't come off."

"Throw it all at his feet Lee. Cast all your worries and cares on him and he will light your path. Lay your burdens down and he will give you peace." Micah said reaching his hand through the bars until it rested on Lee's shoulder. Micah reached into his pocket with his other hand and drew out a small bible. He flipped it open to the book of Ezekiel 37:1-14 and began to read. "The hand of the Lord was upon me, and he brought me out in the Spirit of the Lord and set me down in the middle of the valley; it was full of bones. And he led me around among them, and behold, there were very many on the surface of the valley, and behold, they were very dry. And he said to me, 'Son of man, can these bones live?' And I answered, 'O Lord God, you know.' Then he said to me, 'Prophesy over these bones, and say to them, O dry bones, hear the word of the Lord. Thus says the Lord God to these bones: Behold, I will cause breath to enter you, and you shall live. And I will lay sinews upon you, and will cause flesh to come upon you, and cover you with skin, and put breath in you, and you shall live, and you shall know that I am the Lord.'

"So I prophesied as I was commanded. And as I prophesied, there was a sound, and behold, a rattling, and the bones came together, bone to its bone. And I looked, and behold, there were sinews on them, and flesh had come upon them, and skin had covered them. But there was no breath in them. Then he said to me, 'Prophesy to the breath; prophesy, son of man, and say to the breath, Thus says the Lord God: Come from the four winds, O breath, and breathe on these slain, that they may live.' So I prophesied as he commanded me, and the breath came into them, and they lived and stood on their feet, an exceedingly great army.

"Then he said to me, 'Son of man, these bones are the whole house of Israel. Behold, they say, Our bones are dried up, and our hope is lost; we are indeed cut off. Therefore prophesy, and say to them, 'Thus says the Lord God: Behold, I will open your graves and raise you from your graves, O my people. And I will bring you into the land of Israel. And you shall know that I am the Lord, when I open your graves, and raise you from your graves, O my people. And I will put my Spirit within you, and you shall live, and I will place you in your own land. Then you shall know that I am the Lord; I have spoken, and I will do it,' declares the Lord."

Lee begin to feel something deep within his heart. It was as if there were two hands on his shoulder Micah's and then another's. He felt all the loneness and pain wash away until all that remained was a calmness unlike anything he had ever felt before. It was then that he found a voice to speak.

"O' Father I have failed you so many times. O' the sadness that I have caused you. O' the pain I have inflicted on you. Forgive me father for hating you. Forgive me for turning from you. Forgive me for all that I have done or will do that was and is dishonoring to you. Father forgive me."

Suddenly, there was a loud commotion outside both Lee and Micah heard it. Micah rose to go see what it was, and when he came back Lee could see a look of concern on his face. The door to his jail cell swung open, and he could hear a voice inside him say "Trust and follow me." Nobody stopped him as he walked out of the jail cell and outside on to the street.

CHAPTER 9

A man suddenly burst into her office. She had been watching the commotion in the street and only at the last second turned around. He was a tall man wearing a red cape. She only saw him a moment before he fired two shots. Her body slumped to the floor lifeless.

* * *

He walk down 27th before he turned on to 2nd Ave. North. On he walked until 45 minutes had passed, and he could see the Yellowstone River flowing fast in front of him. Why was he here? What was it that compelled him to this place? That's when he saw them. They were standing by the road overlooking the river. He could see four men and a girl. He knew he was in trouble the closer he got to them. The little he saw of her he knew the girl was Sam, the niece he did not even know he had until a couple of days ago. He suddenly felt stupid for leaving her there at the hospital. He should have known that they would use her to get to him.

"Sacrifices have to be made. You're one of us Lee. You should have known that." Hermes said as Lee got closer to them.

For the first time in his life he was afraid. Deathly afraid. There was Hermes. There was Cicero in his red cape. There was in his midst the very presence of evil. He had no gun. No weapon of any kind. He had tried to reclaim what was his but had failed. Cace dead.

Sister wounded. Niece held captive. Where had it all gone wrong? Suddenly, he heard the voice again say to him "Trust me." It was at that moment that he felt free. Freer then he had ever felt before in his life. God would see him through this terrible ordeal. God not him was in control. All he had to do was fall on his knees and ask God for his help.

"Alright..." He heard himself say. "...let the girl go you have me now."

He watched as they took off the hood that was over the girl's head. She slowly walked past him. She looked up only briefly. In that moment he saw what he had saw 10 years ago when his sister was raped by his step-father. The loss of innocence in the eyes. He knew her life would never be the same after all this. He knew that she did not know who he was. He may not ever see her again. He knew that as is the case with all rape victims that she would evitable blame herself for what happened to her. In that moment he wanted her to know the truth. His words might not make a difference in her life but he had to try and give her hope. His thoughts went back to that night after he had killed his step-father. After he was tired of watching his sister get abused time and time again. He did not have the words then but he prayed that he would have the words now.

"You do not know me. But I know you. You may think that what has happened here is all your fault. Don't. You may have made some mistakes we all have. The evil that surrounds us is the same evil that has existed for thousands of years. It is a battle as old as time itself. You may think yourself broken, a dirty old rag that is no longer needed. Don't. For I have seen the hand of Christ and if he can touch the heart of a violent old sinner like me then he can touch your heart as well. Restore it back to its original luster. Remember that you don't have to be afraid of the darkness if you live in the light of his truth."

"Live in the light huh? Well priest I want to hear you cry out to your God as you beg for mercy." Hermes said walking up to him. Suddenly, he could feel a sharp jab in his side. Followed by a piercing pain right below his left eye. The beating seemed to go on forever.

Until finally, he could not see out of his left eye and barely see out of his right. It would all be over soon he thought.

"Alright bring him over here." He could hear Cicero say. "And stand him up." But as soon as he got to his feet his knees began to buckle and soon he was on the ground again. That's when he heard Cicero say it.

"The only god here is me genius and you are going to pay homage to me."

However, Lee looked up and saw a strong ray of light bearing down upon him and in front of that light walked an old beggar. As the beggar got closer he could see the holes in his hands and feet and the deep gash in his side. The light was so strong that he tried to block it out but could not. Then he heard it. A deep low rumbling sound that seemed to shake the very bedrock of his soul. Suddenly, he felt the ground beneath him give way. What he saw next amazed him. The four men around him vaporized by the light were no more, and he could feel himself falling. Rocks and chunks of pavement were falling all around him. He knew this was the end, and yet he was at peace with it. He no longer felt any pain and suffering. It was quiet in his soul for the first time in a long time. He hit the water at full speed and suddenly nothing. It was as if he were in a deep sleep for an hour or two. He did not know which. When he awoke he found himself on the river bank watching the water sweep past him and that's when he knew he had been reborn. The voice spoke again:

"Follow me."

* * *

He was on his knees at home in his room. He prayed, "Father I am weak. I am broken restore in me a new beginning. Heal my heart O' God so that I may know the paths that lead to truth and avoid the ones that lead to destruction. Father help me to wait for the bride that you have for me. On the day that our eyes meet help me to be captivated by her beauty, help me to have the strength and the courage to lay down my life for her as you O' Lord laid down your life for the Church through your son Jesus Christ. Father I know that in this beauty lies truth and in this truth lies love and it is by this love that my family will be built in your image. According to your will, and your purpose. Lord I know that through your eyes all life is sacred. At the moment of conception you breathe life where there is no life. You create a heart where there is no heart. And I know father that on the Day of Judgment you will create a new heaven and a new earth and all things evil and unholy will pass away. And you will come as a bridegroom to accept your bride the Church and O' what a joyful day that will be O' Lord. Help me to be a man after your own heart. Help me Father to be captivated by your love. Amen." He was going back to work tomorrow but no longer did he dread the coming morning for he knew he was not alone.

* * *

He knew what the papers were saying. He knew the piece of legislation that was being purposed as he climbed the pulpit. "Remember this dear Christian that though the world around us gets darker and darker and persecution is upon us, and though we are called bigots for standing up for the lateral truth of the bible our Savior is with us always. In 2 Chronicles 20:1-23 the author writes, "After this the Moabites and Ammonites, and with them some of the Meunites, came against Jehoshaphat for battle. Some men came and told Jehoshaphat, 'A great multitude is coming against you from Edom, from beyond the sea; and, behold, they are in Hazazon-tamar' (that is, Engedi). Then Jehoshaphat was afraid and set his face to seek the Lord, and proclaimed a fast throughout all Judah. And Judah assembled to seek help from the Lord; from all the cities of Judah they came to seek the Lord.

And Jehoshaphat stood in the assembly of Judah and Jerusalem, in the house of the Lord, before the new court, and said, 'O Lord, God of our fathers, are you not God in heaven? You rule over all the kingdoms of the nations. In your hand are power and might, so that none is able to withstand you. Did you not, our God, drive out the inhabitants of this land before your people Israel, and give it forever to the descendants of Abraham your friend? And they have lived in it and have built for you in it a sanctuary for your name, saying, "If disaster comes upon us, the sword, judgment, or pestilence, or famine, we will stand before this house and before you—for your name is in this house—and cry out to you in our affliction, and you will hear and save." And now behold, the men of Ammon and Moab and Mount Seir, whom you would not let Israel invade when they came from the land of Egypt, and whom they avoided and did not destroy— behold, they reward us by coming to drive us out of your possession, which you have given us to inherit. O our God, will you not execute judgment on them? For we are powerless against this great horde that is coming against us. We do not know what to do, but our eyes are on you.'

"Meanwhile all Judah stood before the Lord, with their little ones, their wives, and their children. And the Spirit of the Lord came upon Jahaziel the son of Zechariah, son of Benaiah, son of Jeiel, son of Mattaniah, a Levite of the sons of Asaph, in the midst of the assembly. And he said, 'Listen, all Judah and inhabitants of Jerusalem and King Jehoshaphat: Thus says the Lord to you, "Do not be afraid and do not be dismayed at this great horde, for the battle is not yours but God's. Tomorrow go down against them. Behold, they will come up by the ascent of Ziz. You will find them at the end of the valley, east of the wilderness of Jeruel. You will not need to fight in this battle. Stand firm, hold your position, and see the salvation of the Lord on your behalf, O Judah and Jerusalem." Do not be afraid and do not be dismayed. Tomorrow go out against them, and the Lord will be with you.'

"Then Jehoshaphat bowed his head with his face to the ground, and all Judah and the inhabitants of Jerusalem fell down before the Lord, worshiping the Lord. And the Levites, of the Kohathites and the Korahites, stood up to praise the Lord, the God of Israel, with a very loud voice.

"And they rose early in the morning and went out into the wilderness of Tekoa. And when they went out, Jehoshaphat stood and said, 'Hear me, Judah and inhabitants of Jerusalem! Believe in the Lord your God, and you will be established; believe his prophets, and you will succeed.' And when he had taken counsel with the people, he appointed those who were to sing to the Lord and praise him in holy attire, as they went before the army, and say,

'Give thanks to the Lord, for his steadfast love endures forever.'

"And when they began to sing and praise, the Lord set an ambush against the men of Ammon, Moab, and Mount Seir, who had come against Judah, so that they were routed. For the men of Ammon and Moab rose against the inhabitants of Mount Seir, devoting them to destruction, and when they had made an end of the inhabitants of Seir, they all helped to destroy one another." Jehoshaphat's prayer should be our prayer. We should cry out to God in the midst of the battle, and he dear Christian will be our deliverer, there will come a time when the days of evil will pass away. Press on dear Christian and serve your king."

Sammy's Song…

"Set me as a seal upon your heart,
as a seal upon your arm,
for love is strong as death,
jealousy is fierce as the grave.
Its flashes are flashes of fire,
the very flame of the Lord.
Many waters cannot quench love,
neither can floods drown it.
If a man offered for love
all the wealth of his house,
he would be utterly despised." Song of Solomon 8:6-7

The Silent Rag Doll

I stand in her midst
but she doesn't see me.
I talk
but she doesn't listen.
And though I would like to think of her
beyond a silent rag doll
she is stoic in her feelings towards me.

Yet I am still held captivated
by her lovely glances.
Her smile
that lights up the room.
O' the harmful miseries of this world.

I buy her flowers
but all she sees is my stone cold heart.
I rescued her
but all she knows is the cracks in my armor.
O' noxious angel
why do you torment me so?
Chew my soul into fragments and
spit on my boyish fantasies?
Why am I drawn to you?
I am dying away
piece by piece
each moment pursuing your face.
Your hair full of yarn,
eyes two large buttons,
clothes scraps of fabric.
O' beautiful creature
don't kill me with your silence,
don't haunt me with your smiles.
Please just tell me your name.
The badge worn over your heart.
So my soul can be
put to rest.

Waif

In the garden alone she stood,
a transfixed angel surveying the luscious landscape.
Her feet had holes,
her hands deep gashes.
She walked with a pain in her side.
A bird sang in the distance,
followed by a crow that came and perched itself on her shoulder.
An odd couple they were,
as they made their way through the garden alone.

The Church

She was barren
her heart torn asunder.
The world trampled her to the ground.
She became a shadow among the dust.
The demons cast lots on her soul,
and darkness encompassed her universe.
"What is this beauty that I see?"
Said the bridegroom who looked deep into the darkness
and saw the light.
Who cast aside the foundations of man
and built the church on the foundation of Grace.

Refuge

I journey through darkness
alone
to capture
a glimpse of your face.
That sweet bright spot in the day
that forces me to forget my own despairs.

Dry your tears
restore those sparkling jewels
to their rightful shine,
and take you to a safe haven.

A place where
the hands will stop touching
the lips stop kissing
and the eyes stop wandering
over your sacred beauty.
A place where
the shadows will not materialize.
A place where
you will be by my side.

O' yes my love
my truest of life
there is such a place.
Apart from mere fairy tales
it resounds
in the secret place
where true faith
never dies.

It is in the soul
of every migrate wanderer
in the heart of every
unfinished story.
It is hope.
and it is
freedom.

The Declaration of the Father

"I will fight to the end."
Says the man dying of cancer.
"I will fight to the end."
Says the farmer in the drought.
Look into the eyes of man
and you will see strength.
It is those eyes that peer
into the face of hardship and do not blink.
"I will fight to the end."
Says the firefighter in the blaze,
the policeman in the firefight.
"I will fight."
"I will fight."
"I will fight."
"I will fight."
Says the mother trying to make ends meat for her family.
"I have already fought…"
Says the Lord
"…for my children and won."

Crowded Streets

Among the crowded streets I stood.
waiting to catch a glimpse of your face.
Faces not your own passed me by,
walking a crooked path.

Among the sobbing and the screaming,
did I strain to hear
the softness of your voice,
the kind words of faith.
But all I heard was pain.
and for that I too wept.

Among the blowing wind did
I beg to feel your breath.
The warmth it makes my heart feel.
The stillness it places in my soul.
But all I felt was the raging storm,
and for that I felt so alone.

Among the crowded streets
I felt the rays of the coming sun.
Little did I know I only needed to turn,
to see you.

I prayed...

The trail that I sought,
I sought alone.
Just me and God
crossing the waters of the Jordan.
I did not think I would know you.
I did not think I would see your face.
O' the nights I prayed for you.
Praying God would lift you up
from the ashes as he has done so graciously for me.
I prayed that he would give me eyes
to see the beauty that he sees.
I prayed that my actions would be honorable in his eyes
and that the footsteps
I followed would be his.
I prayed that your beauty would captivate me.
That it would bring a new understanding
of that most sacred institution into my heart.
I prayed that the bands of true love
would guide you and me into the valley of the shadow of death
and that we through years gone by
would fear no evil
for he would be our God
the God of man, the God of wife.
I prayed dear beauty unseen
for the day our eyes would meet,
and our story begin.

Purity

Words are useless
though I will try to write
for it is in the depths of loneness
that I cry out to you.
I am anxious to live,
I am anxious to love,
I am anxious to see
the bride you have chosen for me.
But I know that I will wait
for you to reveal that which is to be revealed.
I know that time is but a moment
to you O' God so I will wait.
Give me the strength to wait.
The courage to follow.
What will come will come
what will be will be.
Blessed be your holy name O' God.
Shield me from my desires
hold me captive in your embrace.
Don't let me go
for I will fall for I am so weak,
but you O' God are so strong.
Your love endures forever.
Blessed be the name of the Lord.

The Wedding Feast

The Bride of Christ stands alone,
though sickly and pale
though bent and old.
She struggles on in an amoral world

The Bride of Christ stands alone.
The voices from within grow dim
the luster of her time
tarnished by neglect
She cries out for her Savior,
though her cries barely pierce the night.
O the bridegroom comes for his bride
O see him that rights all wrongs.
O see the light of his divine will shine.
O see don't you see
O wretched world
the second coming of Christ?

A Non-Complacent Knight

A mist settles over the battlefield
a calm prevails over the violence that has occurred
and I grow weary holding the sword,
so I drop the sword.
I grow tired of the shield
so I drop the shield,
but there is an evil bearing down behind me
that I do not see.
O' master will I survive the dark watchmen
who come for my soul?
My muscles have grown lazy
my mind feeble,
but this is the calm before the storm.
The monster's breath I feel on my skin.
His eyes are like balls of fire
burning through my bones.
Many have fallen in this fight.
The battlefield is a graveyard strung with corpses
of the fallen.
Why did I lay down my soul
to be ravaged by the wolves that come like thieves in the night?
Why did I go astray from you my God?
I will pick up that sword again.
I will grasp that shield again.
I will turn to fight
the monster that lies within each of us,
for you are my God.
You are my master and commander.
I give all I have to you my God.

I will flee from complacency and run to you my fortress
my strength.
Even though others may not follow,
I will follow.
While others waiver,
I will stand firm.
Praise the Lion of Judah,
praise the most High God
praise the Savior
that saves my soul from the deep black darkness.
Praise the one who stamps out the darkness
and brings light.
Whose feet I follow
Praise the King of Kings.
and Lord of Lords.
Praise the one
who is worthy above all others.
"How do you praise him?"
Others ask.
I will answer them Lord.
"By fighting the battle that never ends---
the battle for lost souls.
Have you forgotten the battle dear Christian?
Have you grown comfortable instead of strong?
Do you not see the fight that is here?
Do you not hear the call to arms Christian?
Defend your bride the Church!
Defend!
Defend!
Defend!
Defend!
Or be a corpse on the battlefield."

What if we came to you on bended knee and worshiped you in fearful reverence O most high God? What if we treated you like the roaring lion of truth that you are instead of the cute and cuddly stuff animal of fairy tales? O God your church in America is under attack and so few are willing to take a stand against this issue of sexual immorality. You know me Christ Jesus my Lord. You know that I have struggled with this in my own life. How many years did I waste away pursuing my own lustful desires when I should have been pursuing you? But you stepped in and brought me back from the pit of destruction. You continue to restore in me a new beginning, a new birth of freedom. You have given me so much heavenly Father that this book is not enough to say thank you. But I will sing till my voice is hoarse, I will write till my fingers bleed of your praises O' God. Lord let your children proclaim your grace and mercy. For I am a wretched sinner in constant need of your grace. Let the darkness that has engulfed your church shudder at your voice. Lord help us as Christians to follow you with all our hearts and with all our strength. Help us to stand Lord and fight for your bride the church, though the costs are high let us sacrifice it all for you O' God. Be with us Lord as we do battle with the darkness help us never to grow lazy in the faith but be bold in our convictions. Help us to walk in your footsteps which are the footsteps of truth and integrity. Lord help us to create a better future for the next generation of Christians which are our sons and daughters. Help us to fight against the things that undermine their future. We are your servants O' Lord use us to proclaim your glory. In you we trust and only you. In your name we pray. Amen.

Levi Wayne Cook

BIOGRAPHY OF AUTHOR

Levi W. Cook was born and raised in Billings, MT. He currently teaches high school English in Fairview, MT. Levi grew up in the church but did not realize what the doctrines of true Christianity were until he was involved in a car accident and God reawakened in him a new desire to serve and honor Christ. Levi believes that he is a wretched sinner saved only by the grace of God which is found in the death, burial, and resurrection of his son Jesus Christ. Levi encourages other Christians to exam their spiritual lives more closely and make sure that they are putting their faith in the one true God as revealed in scripture and scripture alone. Levi believes in the five solas of the protestant reformation. Levi is an active member in his church and is a proponent of local outreach within the local church.

WORKS CITED

Dickens, Charles. Great Expectations. Penguin Group Inc. London, England Feb. 2009.

Frost, Robert. You Come Too: Favorite Poems for Readers of All Ages. Henry Holt and Company New York, New York. 2002.

L'amour, Louis. End of the Drive: "The Skull and the Arrow." Bantam Book New York, New York 1998.

Roosevelt, Theodore. "Theodore Roosevelt Letter to E.A. Robinson, 27 March 1916". Almanac of Theodore Roosevelt. http://www.theodore-roosevelt.com Accessed July 2, 2014.

The Holy Bible: English Standard Version. Published by Crossway. Wheaton, Illinois 2001.